CONSONANT SOUNDS FOR FISH SONGS

BY TRACI CHEE

Copyright © 2012 by Traci Chee

All rights reserved. Except as permitted under the U.S. Copyright Act of 1976, no part of this publication may be reproduced, distributed, or transmitted in any form or by any means, or stored in a database or retrieval system, without the written permission of the publisher.

The characters and events in this book are fictitious. Any similarity to real persons, living or dead, is coincidental and not intended by the author.

Published by Aqueous Books
P.O. Box 6816
New Orleans, LA 70174
www.aqueousbooks.com
All rights reserved.
Published in the United States of America
ISBN: 978-0-9847399-6-7
First edition, Aqueous Books printing, August 2012
Book design and layout: Cynthia Reeser
Cover art: Ruby Guerra

CONSONANT SOUNDS FOR FISH SONGS

TABLE OF CONTENTS

Fish Songs 9

No Place 30

The Human Organ 40

Down (Down Down) 42

The Flying Fish and the Frying Fish 52

The Fisherman 55

Not the Same 60

Over and Over and Over 64

Derek 116

To Keep Me Awake and Alive 122

Raft 125

Love Songs 139

Things Will Never Wholly Kiss You 146

Anatomy of the Human Heart 149

I Hope You Read This / I Hope You Understand It 172

The Wishing Fish 176

Philematophilia 186

Acknowledgments 202

FISH SONGS

The day before Jeffrey A. Whetstone turned into a fish, he was a fully functioning, though somewhat inebriated, human being. Twenty-four hours later he was moving slowly along the bottom of the bay, swimming under the green hulls of boats and between empty nets. He was flicking his fins, dodging Ziploc bags and the occasional amoeba of fuel oil, black glinting purple as the dock lights struck it and glanced off into the depths. He wriggled his slim, slick body this way and that, as he had once seen on the Outdoor Living Network, though TV was quickly becoming a slippery concept, sliding out of his grasp before he could turn it over in his little fish brain.

A note about Jeffrey A. Whetstone: Sometime soon, while slurping algae off a pillar at Pier 17, he will remember that he loved, once. He loved like a human, consciously, but he will never love like that again, if he loves at all. He won't know what to do with his new body, his gleaming scales, the fact that he can't hear sound these days, only feel it.

Seven hours before Jeff turned into a fish, he was sitting in his friend Gabe's apartment, slowly emptying the twelve-pack of beer he had placed on the floor next to him. The apartment was a small one-bed/one-bath white-walled box with a kitchen and cable. Since Jeff had moved in, it had become strewn with paper—pages and pages of it crumpled in corners and scotch-taped to the walls. The recycling pile had doubled in size, and no matter how many times Gabe redeemed it for a pocket full of quarters, it continued to grow.

When he got home that afternoon, Gabe jiggled his keys loudly in the lock, which sometimes stuck, before entering. Slinging his bag over his shoulder, he hefted his bike, a slim thing with smooth tires, and shoved it awkwardly through the doorway.

"Pop quiz," Jeff said from the couch. "Why are eggs the shape they are?"

The corner of Gabe's mouth twitched as he leaned the bike against the wall and closed the door. The kitchen stank—probably food in the drain or dregs of beer in the cans littering the counter. Gabe unbuckled his helmet with one hand, and with the other lobbed a few cans at the cardboard box that served as their recycling bin, missed, and set his messenger bag heavily on the kitchen counter. He sighed.

"Well?" Jeff asked.

"Because their shape makes it more difficult to roll very far and get damaged." Gabe answered without looking at him. He slipped out of his shoes and placed them by the door, hung up his helmet on the bike's handlebars.

Jeff wagged a finger at him. "A good guess. But actually they're shaped like that because they get pushed out of a bird's ass."

Gabe struggled with his tie. "No, I'm pretty sure I'm right. The egg won't go far if it's oval."

"Fine. Two points for each of us."

"Two?"

"One for both of us for getting it right, one for you for knowing random shit about eggs, one for me for thinking up the game. Everybody wins!" He laughed harshly, though it was more of a cough, really.

Gabe crossed his arms. "Discovery Channel? How long have you been watching this?"

"About ten minutes. You just missed a thing on the top ten deadliest sharks. I came in at number six." He paused. "You know I can't resist a countdown."

"So what's number one?"

"I dunno. Some brown one that eats chicks who do their laundry in their river." He frowned at his half-empty beer. "I wasn't paying attention."

"How'd the house hunt go?"

Jeff shrugged. "It's not about finding a house, Gabriel. It's about finding a home."

"Not well, then."

"They don't make 'em like they used to. And don't tell me home is where the heart is, you cheesy Hallmark fuck."

Gabe sat down on the couch with a sigh, wrinkling a sheaf of papers laid on the cushion. He shifted, pulling pages from under him.

"What're you writing?" he asked, glancing at them.

Jeff snatched them away and shoved them under the couch. "The thing about eggs is that they're a bird's period. Want a beer?" When Gabe nodded, Jeff handed him a lukewarm can and muted the TV. "You eat scrambled period at Denny's."

"Yeah, but if you think about it that way, when you get bacon, milk, and a bowl of fruit, you're eating carcass, boob water, and ovaries."

"Fuck I could go for some bacon right now."

Gabe knew that Jeff hadn't picked up the classifieds or turned on the computer that day. That didn't matter. What mattered was that it was getting harder and harder, during those rare moments that Jeff was sober, to talk to him.

Jeff had slowly been turning into a fish for the better part of two years. It had started with the drinking. Sometimes he would drink so much that his piss made the bathroom smell like a brewery. When he could, Jeff would start early because some nights, no matter how little he ate or how many bottles he went through, he wouldn't be able to get drunk. That's when you'd notice the dark half-moons under his eyes.

Really, it probably started before the drinking, which had only recently gotten incapacitating. It probably started with his smile. Jeff had a grin like a shark. A shark is a kind of fish, right? He had one of those desperate, hungry grins, the kind you see on carnivores who know it's only a matter of time before they starve.

Gabe threw a party the summer after they graduated from college. That was a little over two years ago. A few months before, Jeff began trying to breathe alcohol. And Jeff showed up after he got off work—they had him close that night, scrubbing the floors with a dirty, shedding mop, so he showed up late—and when Gabe greeted him at the door, he looked fine.

He smiled, normally though wearily, and shook Gabe's hand. He asked where the booze was, but everyone asked where the booze was, and wandered off in search of a drink.

But later that night, when almost everyone had passed out or gone home, Gabe found Jeff in the backyard, sitting in a rusty beach chair on a lawn that hadn't been mown in six months, staring up at the sky and tapping his forefinger on his thigh like a metronome.

"I thought you'd left," Gabe said, stuffing his hands in his pockets.

"Nah." Tap, tap, tap.

"You going to crash here?"

"Yeah." Tap. "Maybe."

"You okay?"

Tap, tap, tap, tap. *Tap*, tap, tap, tap. "Yeah."

"Look at me."

When Jeff turned around, he looked okay. Maybe a little pale, maybe a little green around the gills, as they say, but okay. And then he smiled, and that's the first time anyone saw it, that shark smile. Everyone who met him after that just assumed Jeff smiled that way, but people like Gabe, who'd known him since high school, knew different.

"I'm fine," he said.

A note about that night: While Gabe was pouring drinks and the little house was heating up with bodies and loud music and laughter, Jeff realized he smelled like Simple Green. It's not that he didn't appreciate the slightly minty scent of the common household cleaner, it's just that when, mid-toss in a game of Beer Pong, he caught a whiff of his own body odor—always a strange experience—he couldn't recognize himself in it.

A glimpse into the future: Two years later, Jeff will not smell like Simple Green anymore, but he will come home from a double shift with the stench of French fries and bleach sticking to him. He'll have bills from Discover and Visa and Mastercard. He'll have to justify impulse buys to himself or return them in the morning: porch swings for a porch he won't ever have, accordions he will never learn to play, inflatable South Pole penguins wearing scarves and Santa hats that he will never blow up or put out for Christmas. He'll stink like deep fryer and disinfectant, and he'll know it, but he will not shower. He will not pay his bills. He will not sleep. He will always, with timekeeping reliability, curl up in a corner with a pencil and paper instead.

Four months before Jeff turned into a fish, he lost his apartment. First he lost track of rent. Then he lost his keys, and he left one window unlocked so he could break into his own apartment each night when he got home from work. Then he lost his apartment when the landlord slipped an eviction notice under his door, and he moved into Gabe's closet across town.

His coworkers said to him, "Like Harry Potter?"

And he said, "Sure. Like Harry fucking Potter."

And they said, "At least you won't have to deal with the Dursleys."

And he said, "Christ, you don't actually read that shit, do you?"

The closet was supposed to be temporary. But Gabe's closet was big enough for him to throw down his twin mattress, and he lived out of packing boxes converted into sets of drawers, and it was easy enough to turn "temporary" into "indefinitely."

Gabe didn't mind. Gabe would have given Jeff a room in the house he's going to buy with his wife in ten years. Sometimes Gabe would come back to the apartment, and Jeff would be buried in paper. Ever since Jeff moved in, paper had been accumulating in the living room, puddling on the coffee table, then overflowing across the base of the TV and into the bends of the floor.

When Gabe came home that first time, Jeff looked up, baring his teeth, and said, "Paper, paper everywhere and not a drop to drink!" Then he picked up a can and raised it in a toast.

Three weeks before Jeff turned into a fish, Gabe found him sitting in the bathroom with reams of toilet paper unraveled around him, piling up like snow as he scribbled on the cardboard cores.

"Jeff?"

Jeff didn't look up. He was wearing boxer shorts and nothing else, shivering. He'd forgotten to turn on the heater. "Form fits content," he said.

"Does it?"

He drew a line across the tube, his hand shaking. "It's nonlinear, see? You can read it in three different circles."

Gabe crossed his arms and leaned against the doorway. "Like a Venn diagram?"

"A what?"

"It's a way of looking at relationships between things."

"No." Jeff drew a series of dots.

"Yeah, that's what it is."

"No, that's not what *this* is."

When he didn't volunteer further information, Gabe asked, "Did you go to work today?"

"Nope."

"Did you call in?"

"Yes. Fuck, Gabe, I'm not one of your kids."

Gabe taught Language Arts at a junior high school a few miles away. He liked it, admired their arrogance and their posturing. Everyone else he knew had lost that strut a long time ago.

"What are you doing?" Gabe asked.

Jeff kept his head bent toward the bare toilet paper roll, sketching sharpie onto it. "Your kids say anything insightful today?" he asked.

"One told me I should have a girlfriend."

Jeff let out a bark of laughter. "Perceptive little fucker. When's the last time you got laid?"

Gabe's face went red and he turned away. "I'm going to the kitchen. Want something?"

"Yeah get me a beer."

Yanking a can out of a six-pack of Natural Light, Gabe sighed and stuck a glass under the tap, filling it with water.

"What's that thing that kid said the other day?" Jeff shouted from the bathroom.

Gabe took a few gulps of water before answering. "I hate the government?"

"Ha! No, the other thing."

"You can never escape the truth?"

"You can never escape the truth!" Gabe heard Jeff laughing, and his laughter bounced off the bathroom walls. "Fuck. You can never escape the truth!"

A note about Jeffrey A. Whetstone: He wrote symphonies. Movements of arias, sonatas, all of them silent, in his head, so only he could hear. Scribbled out, jotted hastily down when the music imagined itself faster than he could follow. When he could, he surrounded himself with it, curled himself under it the way some people huddle under dryer-fresh laundry, enveloped in reams of notes, bars, rests, keys, shifted into piles that only made sense to him, until the music rose in him like a wave and crashed across the room. A reservoir of unplayed music, stored, tucked away, always unheard.

As far as anyone, including himself, knew, Jeff was only happy in two situations. One, he still had the ability, often but not always, to get foolishly, fun-lovingly drunk. Two, when listening to music, but it was becoming harder and harder to hear it. It wasn't about Simple Green or minimum wage or shit jobs. It was about being unable to hear the rhythm in: "Hello, welcome to Jack in the Box. How can I help you." How he couldn't translate the rattle of change in the register into grace notes anymore. It was about watching mouths moving, and hearing, but not listening, and if listening, utterly misunderstanding. About being able to touch his girlfriend, to run his fingers over her ribs, but being unable to hold her. And it became more and more difficult to struggle against that cocoon of silence.

But there were still rare afternoons when he had nothing to do and a few bucks in his pocket, and he'd buy a ticket to whatever film had been out longest—emptier theater—and listen. He would sit in the dark, picking at his hangnails until they bled, just listening. He wouldn't smile. He would be sober. He would be human.

Eight hours before Jeff turned into a fish, his girlfriend broke up with him. He didn't even get off the couch to shout her to the door.

She called him "lazy" and "asshole."

He called her "bitch-tastic" and "Captain Demando" for lack of more creative epithets.

She said, "Grow up."

He said, "Fuck off."

She said the last six months had been a waste of her time.

He said *she* was a waste of time and then proceeded to ignore her until she left.

She had wanted to make a dramatic exit, but really she just kind of slipped out the door and didn't begin crying until she ran into Gabe in the hallway.

"What happened, Janine?" he asked when he saw her. He propped his bike against the wall.

"I don't know how you deal with it," she said, rubbing the back of her hand across her upper lip.

"With what?" Gabe asked.

"Him." She said it so viciously that Gabe cringed. "I'm sorry," she said.

He tried to smile. "It's okay."

"How do you deal with it?"

He shrugged and leaned up against the wall. "I don't know... You've just got to read between the lines, I guess."

"It shouldn't be that way." She had gotten off work half an hour early and driven across town because she knew Jeff had a morning shift. But then she knocked, and knocked, and knocked, until Jeff opened the door and his mouth was hanging slightly ajar and he looked at her like she was trying to sell him something.

"Hey," he said, and walked back to the couch.

"The boss let me go early," Janine said, stepping into the apartment and closing the door behind her.

"Gold star, full marks."

She frowned, but said in the most light-hearted voice she could muster, "Don't be such a jackass."

"Sure." He didn't look at her.

"What's wrong?" She sat down next to him, curled her legs under her and touched him on the arm.

"The Great White is only the third deadliest shark in the world. That's fucked up."

"Jeff?"

"The fucked up part is that they give it a name like 'Great White Shark,' and maybe he's got all these aspirations to live up to a name like that. You could probably change the world if your name was 'Great White Shark.' But then you're only the third deadliest? What a blow."

"Did something happen this morning?" She reached for the remote. Jeff was either intensely focused on the TV or he simply didn't care. Both were possible.

"Nothing," he said. "I'm going to change my name to 'Great White Shark.' People will say, 'Nice to meet you, Mister Shark,' and I'll say, 'Call me Great.'" He dipped his hand over the side of the couch and it came back holding a can. "Want a beer?"

"No, thanks." Janine muted the TV. "Can we talk?"

He didn't look at her. "We can. But we shouldn't."

"What's bothering you?"

"If I said talking was bothering me, would you cut it out?"

She stood. He didn't. "I don't understand you sometimes," she said, crossing her arms.

"What's not to understand. I want to watch the Top Ten Deadliest Sharks. That seems pretty fucking simple to me."

"I don't understand why some days you say you love me and some days you won't look me in the eye."

"Maybe it'll help if I don't say I love you."

"Is that true?"

Jeff looked at her then, and looking back at him was like looking at a man etherized and carved open. He said, "Baby, I don't love you no more."

Fifteen minutes later, standing across the white-washed hall from Janine, Gabe frowned. "You know that's not true, right?" he asked.

"Then why would he say it?"

"It's easier than admitting he does." He put his hand on her elbow. "You didn't know him before. He was different. There's this husk of Jeff walking around pretending to be him, but the old Jeff is still around, somewhere."

A note about Jeffrey A. Whetstone: He wrote in all of Gabe's yearbooks, "Without music life would be a mistake."

Sometimes, when he and Janine were still together, they would spend entire Saturdays in her apartment. It had been winter then, and they'd spend the day in bed, curled under her down comforter, drinking coffee with Baileys and watching TV.

They were watching a movie from Janine's collection once, something with subtitles, and Janine said, "Are you crying?"

"No." His eyes were closed. "I was falling asleep. Thanks for waking me up."

"You can't sleep through this movie. It's Ang Lee."

He rolled onto his side and buried his face in the sheets. "It's a kung-fu soap opera."

"You wouldn't know romance if it bit you in the face."

"I'd sucker-punch romance if it bit me in the face."

Janine was silent after that, watching the movie with furious concentration until Jeff rolled over again, slipped his hand up over her hip bone, and said, "Who am I kidding. Anything with kung-fu is worth watching."

She laid her hand over his, but still wouldn't look at him.

"But this guy. He's no Bruce Lee. He's not even a Jackie Chan."

"He's Chow Yun Fat."

"Yeah he is kind of tubby, isn't he."

Janine laughed.

A note about Jeffrey A. Whetstone: He got so good at pretending to fall asleep when he started crying that he didn't realize he was doing it anymore. Sometimes he *would* fall asleep, and that usually made life easier.

The night they broke up, four hours before he turned into a fish, Jeff was sober, kicking his legs over the side of Pier 17, jutting out into the bay, with nothing but dark water beyond. It smelled like trash, rotting in the shallows, like salt and seaweed. Gabe was sitting next to him, equally sober. "Not tonight," he said when Jeff offered him a beer. "I've got work in the morning."

"So do I." Jeff shrugged, staring at the waves. They caught the city lights like glowing, deep-sea lures.

"You're not getting drunk tonight either," Gabe pointed out.

"I'm trying."

"Well good luck."

"Thanks." Jeff took another drink. "You know what?"

"What?"

"I should have been a pair of ragged claws, scuttling across the floors of silent seas."

Gabe looked at him. In the dim light, he could see that the shark smile was gone, and there was only that desperate look to Jeff's flat eyes. Gabe said, "I know."

The night before he turned into a fish, Jeff was awake at four in the morning. He looked down at what he'd written, notes scrambling up and down the staves, and what he had heard so perfectly in his head sounded the same as the melody he'd written the night before, the refrain he'd composed last Tuesday, the notes he screamed over the weekend while pissing on a tree in the middle of a deserted park.

He flung the ream of music across the room. It hit the TV and all its leaves fluttered to the ground in a heap. Jeff rubbed the bones around his eyes. His skin was greasy. He took a shower.

Standing there, with the water striking him in the sternum and running down his chest, he fell asleep. The water ran so fast it rose to his ankles, then his calves. Over the side of the tub and onto the bathroom floor. The apartment filled with water; the couch began to float but the TV was too heavy. Paper rested on the surface like floes of ice.

When Jeff woke, he half-expected to see Noah in the window, sailing by on a trash barge, steering the shallow streets like a gondolier as goats devoured the pile of garbage on which he sat.

Of course, Jeff was still standing, and the water was beginning to run cold. He toweled off and laid himself down in the closet. He stared up into the sleeves of Gabe's coats and wondered what would have happened if he had slipped. He would have cracked his head on the edge of the tub. He would have bled into the drain. Gabe would have awoken three hours later, heard the water running at seven and known something was wrong. He would have checked Jeff's pulse but Jeff would have been cold already. Gabe would have cradled the naked body and folded his hands and bowed his head and sent out a prayer like a message in an origami bird.

Gabe would have called people. The coroner, or whoever, then Jeff's parents, and probably Janine. She would have made a gasping noise like someone had punched her in the stomach.

Gabe would have worn the black suit with the three buttons, not two, because he would have remembered the time Jeff said the two buttons made him look fat. The funeral would have been small, and the casket would have been closed. Gabe would have known, even if Jeff's parents didn't, to throw a party instead of a wake, and people who hadn't heard about the death would have shown up. There would have been a lot of beer, a lot of drinking, and a lot of people passing out afterwards, shirts untucked, skirts askew.

Almost everyone would have forgotten him by morning.

A note about Jeff's morning: He hadn't gone to work. He called in sick. He dug out his CD collections, played them on the stereo as loud as the volume would go, until the speakers buzzed and he could feel the bass while lying face-down on the floor. He listened to the most stirring music he could find, hoping that something in him would resonate, and his heartstrings were not so brittle, and his body did not break.

Five days before Jeff turned into a fish, he and Gabe were playing the Lord of the Rings drinking game to a TBS showing of *The Fellowship of the Ring*. The rules were simple: Whenever the One Ring appeared onscreen, or whenever there was mention of the One Ring, you drank.

"He's saying it, Gabe, he's saying it." Jeff took a gulp of the forty in his right hand and belched, reciting, "It says in the common tongue: One Ring to rule them all; One Ring to find them; One Ring to bring them all, and in the darkness bind them!" He laughed. "That's three. Oh shit, there it is again!"

Gabe dutifully chugged half of his beer. The couch beneath his ass was threadbare, sagging, with holes like dotted eighths from when someone flicked cigarette ash over it.

"Howard Shore won an Oscar for this score," Jeff said.

"You told me."

"Yeah, but I'm a poet and I've got to show it!" He slapped his thigh. "Hey, does it count if they say, 'Stay tuned for more *Fellowship of the Ring*' during the commercials?"

"No."

"Well fuck. Oh wait, there it is again. Drink!"

They took a few gulps, and in the ensuing lull, Gabe asked, "On average, how many hours per day do you spend thinking about music?"

"Thirteen," Jeff answered promptly. "Give or take. How many times have you masturbated at school?"

"None."

"Really?"

"Yeah." They drank. "What's the last thing you wrote?"

Jeff sighed and muted the TV for the commercials. "Synth lead for a symphony in A major. If you had the choice of fucking a good-looking dwarf or a chick with one eye, which would you choose?"

Gabe laughed. "That's a fucked-up question."

"You bet."

"Do I love her?"

"No. You don't get off that easy."

"Good-looking dwarf. Why don't you play your music anymore?"

Jeff looked at him out of the corners of his eyes. "We should make a rule banning dumbass questions." He looked away again.

"We haven't yet."

"Fine."

"Well?"

"Because it sounds like shit."

The commercials ended. Neither of them moved to unmute the TV.

"How do you know if you don't play it?"

"Because I hear it in my head. It all sounds like shit." He sighed. "One Ring. Drink. Okay: How come you don't keep your nose out of my fucking business?"

"Because I make the rules in this house and the rules say I can put my nose wherever the fuck I want."

Jeff unmuted the TV as the One Ring fell onto Frodo's finger. They both drank. "Fair enough," he said. "I motion to make a rule banning dumbass questions."

"Veto."

"Fuck you."

Gabe chuckled. He ran his fingers along the edge of the couch and took another drink before he asked, "Why does it sound like shit?"

Jeff shrugged. "I don't know."

"Rules of the game," Gabe reminded him.

"I don't fucking know, alright? I don't know. I don't know I don't know. Why do you care so much anyway? You're tone-deaf."

"You're just so unhappy these days."

"Yeah. Well. That's life."

Gabe looked over at him. "No, it's not."

Jeff pointed to the TV. "Drink," he said.

Three hours before he turned into a fish, Jeff was on the bottom of a rowboat kissing a woman whose name he would not have remembered the next morning, even if he had still been human. The floor rolled beneath him. No, that was a woman, and he was kissing her in sloppy, open-mouthed kisses. She was drunk—he could smell it when he came up for air—but he was not. He had her pinned to the bow with his body, awkwardly leaning into her while he braced his feet under the middle seat. The night was on his back, cold and slightly damp, coating him with a chill that coaxed goose bumps to the surface of his bare arms and neck. He wondered if he could see the stars.

He grabbed the woman around the waist, felt her abdomen tense up at his touch, and rolled. The rowboat tipped, letting a sliver of water over the edge, before Jeff was on his back, holding the woman on top of him. She laughed, positioning herself between his legs, and lowered her mouth over his. He raised his head at the last second so her lips closed over his jugular, and around the rim of her ear, he could see the sky.

No stars, not that night, just ambient light making the sky mauve, not black, not even dark.

The water was under him now, icy, seeping into the seat of his jeans and the edge of his T-shirt, and though he was losing feeling in his fingers and toes, he could feel the rowboat rocking every time the woman on top of him shifted.

She bit him, sunk her teeth into his earlobe.

"Ow." Jeff took her by the shoulders and held her at arm's length. "Fuck. What?"

In the dock light, she had yellow skin and slimy lips. She looked at him hungrily and clutched at his shirt with her fingers. "What?" she said.

"Look, Tyson, I don't want to be eaten tonight."

"I do." She laughed.

Jeff flung his full weight against the side of the rowboat and dunked them both into the bay. The woman screamed, then gurgled as saltwater flushed down her throat. She floundered back to the surface, wiped the water out of her eyes and said, licking her lips, "Come and get me while I'm still wet."

She began breast-stroking toward him, but he ducked beneath the surface. The dock light, distorted, made spiderwebs on his skin. Jeff looked up. He was cocooned by sheets of water, comforters that pillowed around his body. His mouth opened and closed, soundlessly. He began to sink, watching the surface fade from sight.

He wondered how long he had been underwater. Maybe three minutes, but that was too long, and as he thought this he took a breath and the water tore through his mouth and out behind his ears.

Breathing underwater became painless after an hour, and he could touch the edges of his new gills without feeling the sting of open wounds.

He felt awkward and heavy, there with his feet in the mud, waving his arms to keep from drifting as scales sprouted over his skin like armor. His legs fused together. His palms lengthened into paddles, slowly—it took maybe two hours but it was getting hard to keep track of time.

He lost his fingers, his opposable thumbs. They fell off, one by one, painlessly and without complaint.

The water was quiet. He listened, but he couldn't find a note, couldn't find a melody in it, though he could swear one was there.

*

Four hours before Jeff turned into a fish, he said, "I should have been a pair of ragged claws, scuttling across the floors of silent seas."

Gabe said, "I know."

"Janine and I broke up." He kicked a can into the water. It landed with a flat metallic sound and bobbed on the surface.

"I saw her leave."

Hand poised on the silver tab of his next beer, Jeff paused. "Was she crying?" he asked. He popped the can open.

"Yeah."

"Shit." He put the can to his lips, then set it on the splintering planking beside him. "Shit," he said.

Gabe nodded. He tipped Jeff's beer into the bay with his index finger. The liquid made a gulping sound as it left the small mouth of the can. "Hey," he said. Jeff didn't say anything, just stared out across the water. "What'd you say to her?"

For a moment, he thought Jeff would change the subject, say, "You know that part in *The Matrix* where they take out power to the entire city? We should do that." But instead he said, "I told her I didn't love her."

"Is that true?"

"No."

"You should call her."

Jeff shrugged, popped the seal on another can, and said, "You know what I should do? Find a fucking party. Someone's got to be doing something tonight."

Gabe sighed so heavily Jeff could feel it on his shoulders. He didn't look up when Gabe stood and said, "I'm going home. You should come with me."

A note about Jeffrey A. Whetstone: He was alone. He was inexplicably, terribly alone, and he didn't know why. Maybe he had been alone his entire life, and only now did he realize it. He wanted to say something, anything, to bridge the gulf opening between them. But he didn't.

At dawn the next day, Jeff was near the surface, trying to breathe. He flung himself up out of the water—for a few brief moments to strain his nonexistent ears for the roar of ocean, the clatter of traffic or the blaring of horns, the pulse of a helicopter's rotors, or even the scream of a gull. But when he left the water, his lungs shrank, withered, and he landed flat-smack in the bay again, after hearing nothing.

His brain hadn't yet figured out how to translate vibration into sound. He wanted to say, "Beethoven," but he could only form the *buh* syllable with his fish mouth.

He wondered what Gabe was doing. Gabe would have woken up by now, realized that he hadn't come home. He would be worried. He would speak to Janine on something called a phone.

He wondered if he could send them a message. If he still knew how to write, and if he could find a Gatorade bottle somewhere near shore, and a scrap of paper, and something to write with, he might write something profound, something that would assure them he was still alive, and maybe he could find his way up the sewer pipes to them.

The message would be carried to the beach by the tide, picked up by a beach comber, who would read the address and deliver like a pizza boy.

Jeff missed pizza, but had no appetite for it anymore. He didn't think he could write anymore either, even if he had the paper to do it with. He missed paper, but now it made him think of the little flakes at the top of goldfish tanks, and it made him hungry.

He spent days starving on algae and being fed saltine crumbs from tourists on the pier, their blurred faces only circles of flesh against the sky. At first he tried speaking to them, but he couldn't hear himself, so he didn't know if he was speaking at all, or just making fish sounds.

Swimming wearily towards the pier where he'd last been human—he remembered its location for about three days before he forgot it—he saw Gabe and Janine standing there, or he thought it was them; he couldn't be sure. But the woman was on her knees clutching the edge of the dock with her fingers. She looked like she was screaming. She looked beautiful. The man was rubbing circles into her back—smooth, rhythmic circles.

Jeff leapt out of the water. He choked, but there was sky, and they were clear, and it was them. It had to be them. The man looked up, but too slowly, and saw only the ripples where Jeff had landed on his side.

They stayed there all day, and he stayed with them. The woman stopped screaming eventually, and she hung her legs over the side of the dock and looked at the water. Jeff swam below her.

She said something to the man. He could see her mouth move, make human sounds. She pointed at Jeff.

The man looked at him then. The corner of the man's mouth twitched. They stared at each other for a long time before the man said something back to the woman.

She nodded.

He nodded.

Jeff nodded, though they couldn't see him do it, and the three of them stayed there until the night came and he felt weak from hunger, and the humans stood, and with last glances into the water, left the dock.

Months after Jeff turned into a fish, he'd forgotten the taste of Chinese take-out but he remembered that he used to like it. He thought of Philly cheese steaks and meatball subs. He thought of fish and chips and felt like a cannibal, but he hadn't eaten anything all day.

Then, as mysteriously as he had turned into a fish, he got the music back.

It began with the waves. He was floating listlessly on his side with one eye towards the sky, bobbing up and down as the waves washed toward shore, sweeping over him and carrying him up, up, then down again. This rhythm he'd forgotten. This beat of footsteps sending shivers down the struts of the pier and into the water, sending ripples across the surface to the edges of his fins. He flipped upright.

He could feel the waves crashing against the beach. Against far-off shores oceans away and the feet of cliffs as they stood by the sea. He could feel the surf pounding—*bam*, bam, bam, bam.

Buh, buh, buh, buh.

Fishing lines dropping like notes, sinking smoothly into the water. Diving birds in the delta, making the reeds quiver. Kids skipping rocks upriver. Plink plink plink—triplets over the surface—while the current hummed over wet stones. Feet and ankles dipping into the shallows, changing the timing, making the melody swerve around skin.

Jeff laughed. He'd never tried leaving the bay before... Fuck, did he leave it now! He had to move! He was fast! He was faster than a speeding locomotive, or at least he felt like it as he left the slow currents behind, skimming through them, dipping in and out of them like a bow singing over strings, with the water on his scales and vibrations in his wake—zip! God he was fast! He was a virtuoso in the water, quickfast like silver.

The current spit him into open ocean and when he came out he was still laughing. He hadn't thought he could still laugh, but there he was, chasing his tail and laughing. He rolled over as the tide pulled him beachward, then rocked upright as the tide pushed him seaward. This rhythm.

He leapt out of the water and he choked on the taste of air but when he fell back in he made a sound, and the sound reverberated across the sea.

He wanted to write it down, but he'd forgotten how. Synth lead for a symphony in A major. He didn't remember synths or symphonies. He wanted to have someone else hear it, to play the lines approaching breakpoint, dodging surfers who complicated his key signatures, to have someone standing on the beach listening, to have her smile. She would drop tears onto the sand. The hush sound of them being absorbed by earth.

He wanted to hold her hand again, and he didn't know who she was, but he could feel her hands in his, ten articulated fingers drumming on the backs of his palms. He wanted to hear her voice, imperfect, throaty, each word encapsulating him like a bubble before bursting and setting him free. If he could have spoken he would have told her he was sorry.

He missed speech. He missed sound and the plucking of notes on frets, harmonics, and the strumming of strings. He wished he could walk, and see his footsteps on wet sand, and if he could talk he would sit with his elbows on his knees, facing the ocean, and someone would say, "You okay?"

And he would be looking at the crests of waves catching sunlight, and he'd say, "Yeah."

Someone would say, "Look at me."

And he would turn, and he would smile and say, "If you had to fuck only one person for the rest of your life, but she was this half-breed mutant, would you want her to be fish on top or fish on bottom?"

"Bottom."

"But then she's got no vagina."

"But she's got a face and hands. And a voice. Why, would you want her to be fish on top?"

And he'd look down at his fingers. And he'd say, "No."

Jeff looked toward the beach, kept his little head half-in and half-out of the water so he could breathe. He imagined sitting there, with the sand getting into his pants. He imagined having pants. And then, slowly, he ducked beneath the surface again, and the pianissimo of water through his gills, and the diminuendo of sun into sea, and rumbling basso profondo in the depths.

NO PLACE

The rules of Jeopardy! were simple. For three consecutive correct answers *or* one correct Final Jeopardy! answer, a player earned the right to bestow upon another player one beer bong. Such rules were recorded in Lion's unkempt scrawl on a sheet of notebook paper magneted to the refrigerator door next to the Domino's coupons and the failed exam scantrons.

In the living room Lion was answering faster than he could think—a desperate attempt to prevent Tiger from scoring three in a row. Tiger was dipping a plastic brush into a bowl of hair dye and running it over his black stripes because his number one fear was the fear of going prematurely gray.

"I'll take 'Good By' for six-hundred," said a contestant.

The screen went blue as Trebek's voice read, "Uninvolved onlooker or—"

"Bystander," Tiger said. He only looked up from his mirror to read the questions. This was the secret to his success; he read and processed faster when everyone else was still listening to Alex Trebek's soothing yet erudite intonations.

"You can't do that," Lion protested from the armchair. He pawed at his mane with an afro pick, a flimsy thing in his king-size claws. "You have to wait for him to finish reading the question."

Tiger opened his mouth and his fangs gleamed immaculately white. He leaned his head back and roared, "Bear?"

"Answer when you want," Bear called from the kitchen.

"Fuck you guys," Lion whined.

Bear scratched his stomach. His claws made a dry scraping sound and he raised them to his muzzle for examination. He had to bring them right up to his snout before they came into focus. Staring at the computer screen at two in the morning was ruining his eyesight. All that hunting and pecking at the keyboard with the tips of his claws, which were flaking at the edges anyway. When was the last time he had sharpened them? Dug them into the bark of a tree?

He opened the cutlery drawer in search of a butter knife, but except for a few bottle caps, it was empty. Grumbling, he shoved the drawer closed and turned toward the sink. The linoleum stuck to the pads of his feet. All that beer sloshing out of cups and cans Thursday through Sunday nights. The sink was piled past its brim with stinking dishes grimy with ketchup and bits of chicken gristle clinging to them.

Bear curled his thick lips and plucked a butter knife from the heap with the tips of his claws. He opened the tap and didn't wait for the water to warm before rinsing and rubbing the blade with a suspiciously brown sponge, rinsing again and wiping it on his belly fur.

He was making a peanut butter and honey sandwich. Three years ago, back when he was still in Wyoming, eating out of dumpsters and using his considerable intellect to gather bear bags out of the trees like fruit, he wouldn't have guessed that he'd end up here, in Santa Cruz, California, studying Anthropology at a university and living in a house with two zoo-born carnivores.

"Get the hell out here, Bear!" Lion cried. "He's got two already!"

Having finished slathering the peanut butter, crunchy, onto a slice of Wonderbread, Bear dumped the knife back in the sink and loosened the top on the bottle of honey. The kind shaped like a bear. Buy one get one free.

"Department of the Interior," Tiger declared. "Next commercial break, you're taking one."

Lion moaned. Bear squeezed honey onto his sandwich and slapped the two halves together. They made a squelching sound and Bear felt goo ooze onto his paws. He collected his plate and, licking his claws, lumbered back to the living room.

"U.S. Cabinets for eight-hundred."

"There you are," Lion said. "Tiger's killing me."

"The minority business development agency," read Trebek.

Bear, halfway through the first bite of his sandwich, opened his mouth but the sound that came out was more growl than English.

Tiger swept the brush over his facial stripes and said, "Commerce."

"Bear said it first." Lion pointed with an extended claw. "I heard him."

"Whatever."

Bear looked out the front window. There was still some daylight left. He might go for a walk. To the beach, maybe. Sometimes Lion and Tiger stayed in the house all day, after partying all night and sleeping past three in the afternoon, and they started to smell like stale beer and the mold growing on their bathroom wall, like unwashed sheets with the faint scent of semen or vomit on them. Bear needed to go for a walk.

But he gulped the last of his sandwich as he walked halfway upstairs, holding the funnel part of the bong aloft as Lion heaved himself out of the armchair and stalked to the kitchen for a can of beer.

"Final Jeopardy! category's 'American Authors,'" Tiger said from the couch.

"F. Scott Fitzgerald." Lion tossed Bear the can.

"Goddammit, I was going to say Fitzgerald," Tiger said. "I've got Cormac McCarthy."

"Faulkner," Bear said, looking at Lion, who just nodded and held the tube to his mouth as warm beer rushed down his throat.

He coughed and foam flew from his lips. "I fucking hate you guys," he said wearily, wiping his mouth with the back of his paw.

The correct answer was L. Frank Baum, which none of them guessed, even with the clue. Bear left before Wheel of Fortune started, and outside the asphalt was warm and slightly sticky under his claws. The evening smelled like seaweed and dead fish, like eucalyptus and the last of the blackberries rotting on their vines, like deer bounding unchecked across campus grounds.

Sometimes Bear had the urge to chase them, to run after them, but one of the caveats of his admission to the university was that he would have to curb all hunting activities, unless in possession of a permit, and only during the authorized season.

His neighbor was watering the plants, green hose sending a jet of water into the air and separating into rainbows. He waved. Bear, ambling down the street on all fours, nodded in response. The college and the locals knew him, even liked him; it was the out-of-towners he had trouble with. When he crossed Mission Street to get to Safeway, they stared or screamed or called the cops, who had to patiently explain that the grizzly bear they reported was a valued member of the Santa Cruz community, a volunteer language arts tutor at the high school and a ladler at the soup kitchen.

Conscious creatures were rare. Back in Wyoming, Bear hadn't known of any others who could even begin to grasp the rudimentary principles of basic middle school algebra, much less get their heads around Ptolemy or Heidegger or Lao Tsu. In fact, Bear had thought himself one of a kind until he met Lion and Tiger, though if he was honest with himself, he wasn't convinced that they were entirely conscious either, at least, not always. Sometimes in the middle of the night, Lion liked to watch Animal Planet at peak volume, drooling at the slow-motion lady lions racing across the Savannah, their muscles rippling beneath their skin and fur.

There was something strange about Lion and Tiger, but it wasn't that they liked to masturbate during the mating scenes on the Discovery Channel. They'd been born in zoos; Lion was from Philadelphia and Tiger was a northern California native, from Oakland. Sometime during his first week in the house, Bear had said, "Did you see how many deer there were on campus today?"

Lion and Tiger were, as usual, in the living room, slouched in front of the TV. Comedy Central was airing features on Chris Rock. This time he was *Bigger & Blacker*.

Lion yawned. "So?" he said.

"So!" Bear cried. "There were five of them just wandering around near the East Field House!"

"Yeah, they do that," Tiger said. He sounded bored.

"Doesn't it drive you nuts?"

Tiger shrugged. "You get used to it."

"Besides," Lion added, "you'd be expelled if you tried anything."

Bear slumped onto the second couch, dropping his book bag on the floor. "But they're just... *there*. They don't even know they should run away when I walk by. You know what one of them said to me today?"

Tiger flicked the tip of his tail and didn't respond, but Lion scratched his belly and said, "They always say 'nice day' to me, even if it's not. They're not very smart."

"They're downright *tame*," Bear said. "And so *slow* too. I bet I could—"

"You know what?" Tiger interrupted.

"What?"

He paused. His pupils focused into black pinpoints in the bright amber of his eyes. He looked like he might have if he was doing calculations in his head, or if he was watching prey move from behind a screen of trees. But then his face relaxed again, and he licked his lips. "You're not in Wyoming anymore," he said. "You're in California now. Get used to it."

"We've never been hunting," Lion explained as Tiger turned back to the TV. "What's it like?"

"Like nothing else," Bear said, trying not to look at Tiger, trying to ignore Chris Rock. "Death is *right there*, you know, so it makes life just as immediate."

"Doesn't it bug you that you can talk to your prey before you kill them?" Lion paused. "And then eat them?"

"Are you thinking of becoming a vegetarian?" Bear asked.

"I've just never gone hunting. I don't even know if I know how."

Bear grinned. "You know how."

"But you didn't answer my question."

"Yeah, no, it doesn't bug me," Bear said, "though I don't know why."

As Bear reached the corner of Nobel and Alta Vista, someone shouted, "Hey shithead!" Bear paused. A gray squirrel darted past him, chattering, "Douche bag! Dickwad!"

Before Bear could answer, another squirrel raced into the street. She fanned her tail and presented her hindquarters before scurrying off again. The first squirrel leapt after her, calling, "Hey baby if I said you had a nice body, would you hold it against me?"

Bear sighed and shook his head. It would have been nice to say not all squirrels were like that, but the truth was that squirrels, chipmunks, shrews, and all other small mammals were just as pea-brained as humans always believed them to be. Little animals with no more room in their bodies for anything besides hunger, sex, and gossip.

It was like that with other animals. Bears are solitary creatures by nature but back home in the Midwest, the elk and deer shied away from him; the cougars considered him competition, snarling and taunting him when they could; and the moose were just fucking mean. Three years ago, living in the woods without anyone to talk to, he was lonely, and when he was offered the free ride to a four-year university, he took it.

He had been picking through the trash of a UCSC Biology professor, who was on a camping trip with his family in the Big Horn Mountains, when they struck up a conversation about the ecosystem and what campers, with their Ziplocs of trail mix and their canned tuna, were doing to it.

"It's not interfering with your natural survival tendencies?"

Bear laughed. "Our natural survival tendency is to get food the most efficient way possible. What interferes is when a bear's relocated. You know what a bitch it is finding your way back from another state?"

"It must be tough," said the professor, offering Bear a packet of instant oatmeal. "I couldn't even find my way here with GPS."

"Thanks." Bear slit the package delicately with the tip of his claw and tapped the oatmeal into his mouth. "Polaris isn't part of Ursa Minor for nothing," he said, exhaling a whiff of cinnamon powder.

The professor tilted his head to one side. "You're pretty smart, for a bear."

Bear snorted. "You're pretty civil, for a human."

The professor explained that UCSC was already hosting two other carnivores—"Think of them as really foreign exchange students," said the Dean of Admissions—so it was a simple bureaucratic process to get Bear enrolled as a freshman for Fall semester.

It was harder to stand in line at the Santa Cruz County DMV to get himself a California ID card, but hardest was the trip out west. Bear had to go by trailer, hitched to the back of a truck, and about three miles out he discovered that he got terrible motion sickness. The nauseating way the vehicle rolled out from underneath him. The whole enclosure stunk of vomit by the time he was let out again.

Now, when he wasn't hunched over his laptop poring through article databases or writing research papers, he liked to sit out by Steamer Lane and watch the waves thrash against the rocks, gnawing at them with white froth teeth. The ocean could kill you. Maybe it was the uncertainty, though certainly you could step off the curb on Soquel Drive and be mowed down by a careless driver, but if you looked both ways and waited for the green light, you could reasonably narrow your chances of dying, whereas in the water you were at the whim of some greater Order, or Chaos, who knew? Bear only knew it was dangerous, and he liked that.

When he got to the beach, the tide was coming in, coming up over the kelp-covered rocks and spraying high into the air as it hit the cliffs, like it was spitting in the sky's face. Bear smiled, and some woman with a stroller squeaked audibly and wheeled quickly away from him. Though he would never tell Lion or Tiger, who thought of "the wild" as a bigger, more complicated zoo enclosure, Bear missed Wyoming. It was crowded here, where the houses had small manicured yards and the people jogged down West Cliff with iPods clipped to their arms, where lines of cars cut the city into pieces. There were even people in the woods, who built their houses in trees and didn't wash their hair, and they too were afraid of Bear when he wandered into the forest. They were so afraid, all the time, of everything, and there was nowhere to go to be alone with the smell of the earth under your claws and the freedom of rolling naked on your back in a patch of clover.

The sun dropped into the ocean and doused the sky with orange and pink, so the clouds and leftover jet streams were saturated with it. Surfers in wetsuits began climbing onto the beach, dripping like half-human, half-animal hybrids. They shook their heads and droplets of water flew out of their hair. Bear remembered what it felt like to shake the river out of his fur: lightening and empowering.

The ocean was rising, throwing itself at the land, like it could tear down West Cliff and the houses perched on its edge, like it could reclaim its territory. Bear waited until his section of beach was clear before he went down to the water, pausing where the waves lapped at his toes, almost playfully, beckoning him in.

He thought of Lion and Tiger, sitting at home, scratching themselves and saying, "Solve the fucking puzzle, asshole."

He dove into the water.

It was fast, and it was strong. The current tore at his limbs, trying to drag him under, but Bear was powerful, even if it hadn't remembered it until then, and he kicked away from shore, paddling west towards a sun that had already sunk. The motions were automatic, and they carried him far, far from the beach, until the lights on the Boardwalk were only a glitter on the horizon and the stars grew larger and brighter and more numerous the farther he swam. For the first time since he left Wyoming, he felt like he was close enough to the sky to feel it.

Bears don't float. And Bear was getting tired; the more weary he got, the more the ocean weighed on his legs, pulled them farther down with each stroke. He couldn't always see the north star from the cul-de-sac at the end of his street, but he could see it now, glinting faintly among the Dippers.

Bear turned toward shore, little more than a smudge now, and began swimming back. By the time he could feel the occasional algae-slick rock beneath his paws, his limbs felt limp and rubbery. He kept pawing for the bottom, but the water gave way beneath him. Twenty feet to shore.

Something big and smooth brushed up against his belly. Bear swiped out with his claws but they were thick and slow in the water. He looked, but it was so dark down there he could only see reflections on the surface. Something nudged his back legs. He tried to swim faster, but the tide kept pushing him away from the beach.

A creature surfaced a few yards away. Bear hoped it was a seal or a porpoise, but then he saw a thousand white teeth glinting in the light.

"What are you?" the shark asked.

"I'm a bear," Bear answered. He considered his chances for survival. He looked toward land, tried to think of something to say. "What are you?"

"I'm a shark."

"You're a predator?"

"Yes."

Bear thought of Lion, who hadn't been hunting once in his entire life. "Doesn't it bug you that you can talk to your prey before you kill them?" he asked.

"No."

Bear tried to think of Socrates—Charmides, Crito, Euthydemus, Gorgias—but he could think only of the monosyllable: "Why?"

"I'm meant to kill them." The shark swam closer. It was a long, well-muscled creature with black discs for eyes.

"But they beg for their lives." Bear thought of screaming, of squealing, high-pitched and desperate. He began treading backwards; subtly, he hoped, searching for rock with the tips of his claws.

The shark followed him. "Yes they do."

Bear thought of land. He looked toward the lighthouse and the wharf. The whole crescent of the Monterey Bay lit up. He thought of electricity, PG&E bills, street lamps, roads, bridges,

CalTrans, orange cones and traffic jams, infrastructure, overcrowding and overpopulation. "How can you eat them then?" he asked.

The shark seemed to consider this for a minute, staring at Bear without blinking, and then it said, "They are weak, and I am hungry," and sank soundlessly into the water.

Bear thought of the deer, saying "nice day" during fog and rain, heads bowed beneath gray and dripping skies. He thought of them growing fat and complacent and slow. He thought of chases. The crackle of brush. The frantic pounding of hooves. He thought of white tails and fleshy haunches. His paws scrabbled on wet rock. He bared his teeth. Solid ground. He felt his fur bristle. He felt his legs stiffen. He remembered this. His muscles bunched. He loved this. The adrenaline through his forepaws. The sharpness of his claws and the growl growing in his throat. The shark was coming, but Bear was ready. Tear off its fins first. Don't let go. It was a matter of keeping your footing, and that was all.

THE HUMAN ORGAN

You stand in a crowd dark close sound magnet hummmm lull of voices human throats drone, noise in your teeth—

It's about $_{falling,}$ it's about $_{dizziness}$ and the blank step into the spaces between notes, it's about missing the beat and having it come back to you, it's about upsurging and deep places, it's about the sudden blinding burst of light

You stand in a crowd and sweat hot noise ears ringing wet disintegration of your hearing tremor pressed against by bodies leaping into the air all at once school of fish flight on the downbeat ^{the} $_{downstroke}$ the crack of kick bass yeah yeah fuck yeah.

It's about rests. it's about losing things and finding them again it's about being ONE when you're always so goddamn alone, it's about standing in that crowd dark close like a magnet with sparks flying out of your wrists.

THE HUMAN ORGAN

We're not even human anymore we're pipes, set of ribbed red flesh wet on the inside with all that air flowing out of us friction against our insides our chords open so open all that ecstatic uncontrollable
                        Holdit.

sound. Go forever if you can forget measures forgo timing and tempo forget that everything's ending we're pipes remember the human organ the human voice this voice yeah that God created when he looked down at the world and saw how fucking lonely it was without us and then he flexed his fingers he cracked his knuckles and sent solar wind whistling through us cleaning us out and making us scream into the holy abysmal dark to fill it all up it
                                                                             was always about
                making noise.

DOWN (DOWN DOWN)

Once it was about getting noise complaints from the man upstairs. Hello from Heaven, this is God speaking. I know you're all enjoying yourselves down there, and don't get me wrong, that's what I made amplifiers for, but you're making such an awful racket. We can hear you all the way up here, and my cherubs won't stop crying, and none of the seraphim can hear themselves think, and I'm getting the most monstrous headache, so would you please quiet down (down down).

Once or twice or maybe dozens of times we shoved the furniture up against the walls. We stowed all the stuff we didn't want broken—lamps, vases, picture frames—deep in our closets. We stocked the kitchen with booze and bags of chips and microwave popcorn, but mostly booze. We gestured to a corner of the living room and said, "This is your stage!" And later that night, later these nights, when there were so many bodies in the room we were a fire hazard, when the amps and mics and cords were strewn across the floor, when it got hard to breathe, when the music was going and the singers were singing, when the guitars were so loud they were just noise and we were all shouting and jumping and every measure, every count of four was like being reborn, we went *na na na na—yeah!* and right then we all leapt into the air and we were weightless and the laws of gravity no longer applied to us. We were all grinning foolishly as our feet and knees raised up, and we were squatting, but we were squatting in midair, and I gotta believe this, we were flying too, and we were all grinning foolishly and we knew it.

Once I star-sixty-nined Him. Didn't know what I was going to ask, but it was dawn and the morning light had this quality like water. The walls were seriously pounding still, the dishes in the cupboards were rattling still, I had this singing in my ears still, and as I stood there in the middle of our trashed living room, with the snoring sleepers and the tipped-over beer bottles, I felt like I was going vibrato, and it seemed as good a time as any to hear what He had to say, but when He answered the phone (Hello son), I hung up. There was this lingering brightness in the speakers, the preamp outputs.

Once Antonia and I lay siege to the Electronics Aisle. We dialed every clock radio, every boom box, every home theater system to 102.1 and turned that shit up as loud as we could. It came in halfway through something of Bach's. Something with an organ. Music to God.

"Louder!" I shouted.

"What?" she asked.

"Louder!"

She had a rippling laugh. "That's as loud as it goes!"

The whole store flocked to us. They were drawn to us, they couldn't help it. We flooded every square inch of that warehouse from Furniture to Women's Apparel and when the sound hit the sliding glass doors to Outdoor Living, they slid open with a *whoosh* like the deep breath of surfacing.

I've loved Antonia for years. It turns out love is real after all. I know. Holy shit.

It's the little things about her: how she buys shorts with lots of pockets and she puts stuff like Band-Aids and paper clips and safety pins and marbles and crackerjack stickers in the pockets, or how when something is really funny, she laughs with her head thrown back and her eyes closed and her mouth open so you can see all her teeth and the silver fillings on her back molars, and it's not that she's really beautiful then, it's that she doesn't care if she's beautiful because what's important is that she's alive.

I like that she puts up with me. I try to tell her jokes to get her to laugh like that, but it doesn't always work. Like: "Where do one-legged people work?"

I like that I don't have to tell her that I love her because she knows me well enough to know already. Because if I told her, she'd be sad, she'd feel bad because she doesn't love me in a way that she wants me, and I love her in a way that I want her, but I don't have to have her. Because if I had to have her, it wouldn't be real love.

Once while jumping from my couch and shredding the fuck out of an air guitar, I broke my ankle. I fell down (down down) and **snap!** went my bone. I spent two weeks on Vicodin and every minute was fuzzy and small and quivering between my fingers.

Every so often I go to church—there's one on 16th and Broad Street that I like, the one with the sky-blue front steps—not to listen to the pastor or even to pray, but to go sit in the pitted wooden pews and stare at the little pencils and the battered hymnals and the old copies of the American Standard Version, and I listen to the organ. I like how when it swells it lets out this sound like a big wave, and if it gets loud enough, it's like the water rises high over the tallest skyscrapers in the city, over the TV antennae and telephone wires, and for hundreds of miles around—deep into the flat of the desert—you can see the wave rising and rising, ready to crash down and wipe everything clean.

Once I came out of work and the street was the loudest I'd ever heard it. It was past midnight, and no one was around, and the sky beyond the edges of the buildings was black and wet. A block away, from the front doors of the club, the bass was overflowing onto the street, washing away parked cars, dead leaves and empty cups, sharp pebbles of glass, grit in the sidewalk, and when the music collided with my body, I was swept down the road, sailing on the roof of a minivan with damp shoes and my arms out. And then, just then, only then and never again, I thought I heard someone say, *Holy holy holy.*

Once Antonia said, "Let's set things on fire," so we called everyone we knew with shit to burn. We went to the desert. We brought cardboard and old newspaper and Duraflame logs, and we built this pyre out of some old wood pallets, emptied a couple bottles of lighter fluid on it. We struck matches. Everyone scampered back to watch the light blossom out, touching nearby cacti, dry stalks of sagebrush. "Look up," I said. "Look up." It was a pillar of flame in the night. Smoke and our voices rising up (up up).

Once I brought Antonia a pack of madeleines. Her face was pulled down, and there were wet specks on her T-shirt. She said, "You brought me cookies?"

I said, "I brought you cookies."

She took one, and her fingers crinkled the plastic. When she ate it, tiny powdery crumbs fell from her lips onto her shirt. I wanted to brush them away, but I didn't. She was crying.

I took her in my arms. She dropped her cookie on the floor.

Later, I said, "You don't need to worry."

Her head was on my shoulder, so I couldn't see her face. She said, "You don't know that."

"I do, though."

"How?"

The cookie was still on the carpet. It had crumbled when it struck, and where Antonia had bitten it, small pieces had scattered on the ground.

I put my cheek to the top of her head. "He's gone to join the choir," I said. "I've heard it. The choir. You hear the choir and you *know*. That there is a choir. And a conductor who is also a composer, and he's got the music in his head, and he's coaxing it out of everything. You hear the choir and you know that when people are gone, all they've done is gone upstairs. The angels will hand him a book of sheet music, but he'll already know all the songs. What was he?"

"A bass."

"Yeah, and he'll already know all his parts by heart. He'll step into formation with the other basses, and they'll smile at him because they'll already know him, and he'll open his mouth, and when his voice comes out, it'll be like he's always been singing."

"Granddad used to say he couldn't carry a tune in a bucket."

"It's not really about singing, you know."

"Yeah." She pressed the heels of her hands against her eyes. She sighed. "I don't know if I believe all that," she said. "But I'm glad someone does."

Once I wanted to see the dark and the flat. I wanted to have it all around me, so I drove to the desert and parked my car on the side of the road. I got out, and the sound of the door slamming was a thunderclap. I stood there on the warm asphalt and looked up. Did you know there are more stars than you can count and each one is a song and they're all playing up there, so it's never as quiet as you think. Someone is always singing.

Once while crowd-surfing, at one of those venues packed wall-to-wall with sweaty, singing, jumping people whose bodies are filled up with sound, and you're so close to them you forget where your body ends and theirs begin, I leapt so fucking high that I came down upstream and there were all these hands holding me up—

>Sprawling: my face, my belly, my chest to the ceiling—no—*past* the ceiling, straight through the roof to the fucking sky! Lifted, taken up by all those human beings, all those voices, all those heartbeats, all that glorious God-given *sound*. I wanted to be screaming, "Up up up!" (Maybe I was!) We were the great wave rising over the city, over the desert, over the whole fucking *continent*, and I was there at the peak of it, so close to the sky I could hear it inside me.

—and then I wiped out on the concrete floor. Dropped, just like that. Bruises. Boots and shoe soles. The heavy thud of my body on the ground. Everything disordered and dizzying.

Someone pulled me out of the pit but I didn't know who, it was so dark and all those legs were so disorienting, and someone said, "Don't crack." You get these cryptic messages sometimes.

Once I was looking for soap in the Health & Beauty Aisle—I don't know, I had soap, but I needed to feel clean again, really clean, clean and shiny, so that when light or sound struck me, it would reflect and go rocketing off into the dark places and silent corners—and I had my hand on a box of Dove when someone got on the loudspeaker (you know how sometimes you're standing in the Health & Beauty Aisle with brown-flecked tile under your sneakers and this sharp, stale scent like nail polish remover sinking into your skin, and someone interrupts the pop radio and all the sound cuts out for a second, and you're waiting, you're hanging onto that box of Dove like you're hanging on for the next beat/note/chord/snare/cymbal/word, and when it comes you think you can hear it, you think someone's calling your name but their voice is muffled and overrun with static and you can't understand a thing?). It was like that, I was like that, riveted to the center of the aisle, with fluorescent lights flickering on me as I stood there, straining to hear, clinging so hard to that box of soap that my fingers punctured the plastic wrapping, the cardboard underneath.

Once while walking down 11th Avenue, instead of the gutterpunks and the silver salesmen there was a group of hardcore Episcopalians or Calvinists or Jesuits or whatever, and they told me I was going to hell.

They told me, "Love Jesus."

They had signs.

They said, "Repent or perish."

What did they know. I'd heard the fucking choir. I'd heard the fucking *choir*, alright? And even though I knew the answer, even though I knew I did, I still said, "Do I really need my eternal soul anyway."

Then one of them spit on me and have you ever been spit on (?). Like maybe he just had bad aim and missed the sidewalk, but I don't think so.

Once I didn't make it back. I had a splitting headache when I left the venue. My body was aching, not from the fall but from missing the hot electric touch of all those hands on me. Antonia followed me out. She put her palm on the side of my face and asked, "Will you be okay?"

I leaned into her hand. Just a little. Just for a second. So she wouldn't notice. Then I said, "Don't crack."

She said, "What?"

I said, "Yeah, don't worry about me. It didn't hurt that bad."

Then I went looking for noise.

I looked for it outside of work. I shoved my hands in my pockets and walked over to the club. The low notes were coming through the walls. I paid the cover charge, wandered into a throbbing crowd. It was hot and the music was loud. I wanted my pulse to change, to jump—but it didn't.

I looked for it in my car. I dug through the cassette tapes in the back seat, felt them clatter in my hands, spun the little spools with my fingertips. I plunged one after another into the tape deck, cranked the volume until my speakers rattled and my mirrors blurred from the bass.

I looked for it in the desert. I waited for a sound like a thunderclap, but it didn't come. I laid down in the dust—my face, my belly, my chest to the sky—but the earth was cold and hard, and everything was so still. I was so still. It was the stillest I'd ever been. And I saw all these stars, little thorny barbs, but no one was singing. I curled up into a ball.

I looked for it in my kitchen. I took a wooden ladle and banged on all the pots I could find. I took a frying pan to the garage. I hauled our garbage can to the driveway. I kicked it onto its side and pounded at it with the frying pan, with the ladle. I dumped the trash onto the concrete and battered the can with my fists. I was screaming. I was screaming so loud it burned.

When I was done, I sat down cross-legged next to the pile of garbage and cupped my hands over my ears, but I didn't hear any waves, didn't hear any great ocean, didn't hear anything at all.

Once I irreverently struck a chord and broke it in half. "I didn't mean to," I said to its carcass (cold and small and still). "I'm sorry I'm sorry."

Once we were all in our little house, and the floor was moving up and down (down down) with so many people launching themselves off it, blam!, right into the air. It was a temple, it was a church, you could feel the music blocks away, see the light radiating into the night, but I was knock knock knocking on the back door 'cause someone had locked me out, and they couldn't hear me calling.

Once I said, "I love you, okay? Don't you get it I love you."
She was crying. I'd made her cry.
So I said, "So a mushroom walks into a bar, right?"
She said, "Not again."
We'd just left the bar and we were drunk. But I was still thirsty. I felt dry, like a small clod of dirt and I'd crumble the second someone touched me. I'd turn into dust.
She just stood there and cried. Didn't say a word.
So I walked away, and if she called my name, I didn't turn around.

Once I wrote down all the promises I had ever made on 3x5 cards and taped them to my bedroom door. *To be patient. To be kind. Never to envy. Never to boast. To be slow to anger. To keep no record of wrongs. To rejoice with truth. To protect, and trust, and hope, and persevere.* Then I tried to shatter them with a nine-pound hammer, but I missed. There were holes big enough to fit your fist through.

"Mom?" I said.

She said, "I'm glad you called."

"I broke my door," I said. "I hit it with a hammer."

"Oh honey," she sighed. "What happened?"

"I don't know," I said. "I just got so desperate."

"Come home for a few days," she said. "Come stay with me for a while."

I thought of home. I thought of Mom's collection of porcelain angels—with round faces and curly hair and stubby wings, clutching harps or choir books. We both knew angels didn't look like that, but she kept them all the same. I thought of my old bedroom, with trains on the wallpaper, still. I thought of the maroon of my carpet and towers of old CDs stacked in the corner, in the closet, on the bookshelf. I thought of the plain wooden cross mounted above the bed. I thought of being surrounded by all that dusty music, stuff I'd listened to when I was a kid, and I was afraid.

"I can't go back," I said. "Not now."

"You can always come home," she said. "You're always welcome."

"It's not so bad out here," I said. I forced a laugh. I shoved it out of my throat and into the open air. It hung there between us: the ugliest sound I'd ever made, raw and glistening. I wanted to wipe it away. I wanted to swallow it again, but I couldn't take it back. "I'm sorry," I said. "I'm so sorry."

"I love you," she said.

"I can't hear you," I said.

"Hello?" she said. "Can you hear me?"

"I can't hear anything anymore."

"Hello? Hello?"

Once Antonia looked sad so I said, "So a mushroom walks into a bar, right?"

She said, "Is something wrong."

She said, "You look thirsty."

I said, "I am."

And we drank, but we didn't really drink, and I couldn't hear the clink of glasses or the hollow sound of near-empty bottles on the wooden bar, the buzz of ESPN on the TV, the radio... I couldn't hear her voice, and time passed, but nothing moved.

Sometimes these days I stand outside looking up waiting for something to fall (down down down) into my hands.

THE FLYING FISH AND THE FRYING FISH

I. Godlike

If your goldfish goes crazy for Stravinsky, you play him some goddamn Stravinsky. Stick him in a plastic bag and put him on the floor and he can feel the vibrations. Hook up some amps, pop in *The Firebird*, and blast that shit as loud as you can. Rattle some walls. Get some neighbors knocking on your door. Lemme tell you, some of them just won't understand. They'll tell you your goldfish can't appreciate the rhythmic complexity. They'll say he's got a three-second memory. Say he can't follow the changes in tempo. Fuck 'em. Igor stirs something deep down at the pea-sized core of his little fish soul. I mean, just look at him.

II. Brimstone

It's hot. That's the first thing. Then, the pot. It's a motherfucking behemoth of a pot and there are thousands of us standing on the edge of it, pressed shoulder to sweaty shoulder. I look down, and it's like Duck Duck Goose, but instead of a mush pot there's a pit of magma. Someone says, "Eternal damnation," but I don't believe it. Hell couldn't feel this great. I laugh this really big belly laugh that opens me way way up. I laugh so hard I tip over the edge and fall right in. The joke's on everyone else. I burn up before I hit the ground and take off as smoke.

III. Buckshot

I saw a kid once. The saddest human being I'd ever seen. I don't know what it was about him. He had these big brown Bambi eyes and a coat-hanger collarbone, but that wasn't it. He said to me, "Consider it a favor." I don't know what that meant. His mouth was like a broken pencil. I think I gave him a quarter, but he gave it back to me. He said, "No, Nielsen. Adjective function block sets are the world's lost hopes." He was fucking crazy, but so sad. He made me want to cry. I never saw him again.

IV. The Fourth

Visit Phoenix, if you can. I grew up there, called it home. It was so hot in the summer, every house in our neighborhood had a pool, and from above, our streets were dotted with unnaturally blue nuclei. Come July, sun-baked and wet with chlorine, we'd watch fireworks spatter the sky. And lightning. White streaks like angels. When I still believed in angels, you know? Things slow down in heat like that, under skies like that, so even the hot crack of light in the sky lasts a whole night, and you feel like you can watch the entire lifetime of a saguaro cactus silhouetted on the flat purple horizon. You want to stop time so you can drink it all in, soak in it until your fingertips are pale and pruny. It slows down, it comes close, but it ends before you're ready.

V. Deep Fryer

You're probably not thinking when you set up your stereo system in your bathroom, draw a bath, and immerse yourself fully-clothed. You just want to know what *The Firebird* sounds like through water, because it does things to your goldfish, so that he's not even a goldfish but a brilliant, fast-beating heart. Let me tell you, brambles burning on a mountaintop, that's what it sounds like. And when the speakers shake so bad they fall into the tub with you, you fry like an egg on summer sidewalk. You turn to glass like sand struck by lightning and your soul flies out of your mouth, laughing.

THE FISHERMAN

Marianne carries a glass jar when she walks down the street. She carries it with her wherever she walks, watching the sky for the Fisherman. She imagines him appearing between the high-white clouds, bearing a fishing pole in his thick-fingered hands. He will have creases at the corners of his eyes from sun exposure and from laughing. He will wear a floppy bucket hat dotted with hand-tied flies, and he will be smiling.

Marianne has a smile like a Ziploc bag. If a memory is sealed inside her, it will stay fresh for a month. Joe, her lover, fingers the slit of her lips and watches happiness spread from cheek to rosy cheek. He draws it out of her with his breath, licks it from the white snowcaps of her teeth. She lets him. She tilts her chin under his finger; she closes her eyes like a contented cat curled in a puddle of sunlight on his lap.

Joe should remember—though he won't—that she's had fingers curled into her chest, ripping and ripping until her heart spilled onto the floor. An embarrassing mess—she knelt beside it as echoing footsteps stepped around her and out the door. She stared down at it for an hour before retrieving the mop and bucket. You don't know what heartbreak is until you've wrung it from the dreadlocks of the mop and watched your blood mix with the soap suds.

Joe met her while fixing the leak in her ceiling, where the water got in. He liked the serenity in her face, doe-like, and the curves of her cleavage when she held up a glass of apple juice for him as he stood on a ladder with the tips of his hair brushing the ceiling.

Marianne likes to rub pennies against the sidewalk until they shine. She likes the heat of the copper between her thumb and forefinger; she likes the gleam of blank penny in the sunlight. Nickles, dimes, and quarters are less entrancing; she pockets these and spends them on packs of Wintergreen in cramped stores crowded with kitchen wares, where on the top shelves regal or priestly figures with painted faces raise their palms and smile as sticks of incense write eloquent, looping sentences of poetry. Marianne imagines brief prayers that involve antelope and ransom notes, empty cardboard boxes and trains.

She follows the smoke down the street. The sidewalks are wet with melting ice from the fish market and the blood of halved pigs being carried by oily men. Marianne can count ribs. She clutches the jar tighter to her waist and continues past a store with roasted ducks hanging by their necks in the window.

Marianne imagines that when the Fisherman arrives he will cast his fishing line and the tip of it will hover right between her eyes before he flicks it back into the sky again. She will hurry to catch it. She will dodge old ladies in down coats, carrying bags of bok choy in their claw-like hands. The fly will slip out of her reach again, and she will bump into pregnant women with their bellies exposed, the round undersides like glowing peaches. She will trip over the curb and cars will honk, but she will not drop the jar and she will not get hit.

Joe doesn't understand Marianne, but he probably loves her the way he loves dogs and retarded people. She bakes him cored apples stuffed with butter, jam, and a pinch of cinnamon. She waits in front of the oven for forty-five minutes, inhaling that sweet, warm smell. When Joe comes home, she serves him the apple on a plate and drizzles white chocolate chips into its molten insides. She expects him to say thank you, but he might have burned his tongue. He might have a layer of skin peeling from the inside of his mouth like tissue paper.

When Joe gives her the pills she swallows them quickly in a sip of water. Marianne imagines them collecting in the pit of her stomach like pebbles or marbles that gleam in the light when she opens her mouth to laugh, to drink, or to exhale.

Joe should realize—but he probably doesn't—that he can't try to fix Marianne. The last man who tried to fix her took her apart, piece by piece, examined the malformed bits she never showed anyone else, scrutinized them under a magnifying glass at the kitchen table. He left her like that, all strewn across a white tablecloth, her forefinger a crescent around the salt shaker, her tibia leaning against the leg of a chair.

When Marianne goes to sleep one night she wonders why Joe didn't kiss her that morning before he left for work. She breathes into the cup of her hand and sniffs, but all she smells is toothpaste. She gets out of bed, sticks her hand into a pickle jar filled with faceless pennies, cat's-eye marbles and thimbles, and she feels better.

Marianne buys a bag of Fuji apples from the market on the corner, where the fruit tumbles around her searching hands. She examines each apple for blemishes and finds none that are not bruised; some cut open by the edges of the hard wooden crate, some squashed by the weight of other apples. As she pays, she loops the plastic bag over her arm and sets the jar on her hip, cradling it in the crook of her elbow. She counts change in her palm and thinks that she won't have enough money for the fabric store three avenues down.

She will never get to the fabric store. Halfway across the crosswalk, Marianne drops the jar. The top half of it shatters. Marbles, tumbled stones, buttons, pennies spill onto the street. Fragments of glass catch in the cracks of the asphalt, made by earthquakes or car tires or pipe bombs. She stoops to pick up the shards as the stop light turns yellow.

Horns blare.

With the half-jar under one arm, Marianne places the pads of her fingers on one smooth side of a piece of glass. She tips it back into the jar, careful to avoid the sharp edges. When it lands it makes a tinkling sound like water.

People gesture angrily and shout.

As she scoops up a handful of pebbles, Marianne's fingertips catch on the jagged bits embedded in the street. Glittering dust in her prints. She stares.

A gleaming hook drops into the palm of her hand and she is lifted, lifted, lifted into the sky on the end of a fishing line. The Fisherman is just as she pictured, though handsomer, with a jawline like a rock and a well-muscled cowboy body she hadn't expected.

His palm at the meeting of her ribs, her naked body caught in the net of his arms and legs. His mouth at the niche in her clavicle. Her fingers, still stinging, tracing the peaks of his vertebrae, the divots above his ass. He says it's part of the thoracolumbar fascia, and he is smiling.

When the Fisherman returns her to earth, Marianne will come straight home. She will set the jar on the kitchen table. It will have been glued together again by the Fisherman, who peered at it under his fly-tying magnifier and painstakingly set the edges back together. She will wait for Joe to arrive. She will want to tell him the truth. She will explain that it was only once, once only, and never again.

She will cling to his arm when she says this, and he will be overcome with disgust. He will fling her away and say, "Crazy bitch."

Joe will pack his things and leave.

Given a secret, Marianne will seal it by pressing the first finger of her left hand to the bow of her lips. After Joe, she will not tell a soul about the Fisherman.

She will bear a child. Her belly will swell like ripe fruit and her mother will ask her who the father is. Everyone will assume it was Joe, but when contacted, he will deny it, knowing that it will not be his little boy who is born into that quiet midwinter dawn.

His name will be Fisher, after his father. Though Marianne will love him more than all of her collectibles combined, though she will give one to him each day of his childhood—a marble, a stone, a button, a penny—he will not belong here. He will yearn for the open ocean. One day, when he is old enough, he will be striding along the beach in his bare feet, with his pants rolled up to his knees. He will stand in the surf while the tide rolls in and out and in again, tumbling smooth bits of beach glass and limestone pebbles and shards of clamshell around his ankles, and then he will walk onto the water, striking out past the cliff house toward open sea. He will place his heels on the surface, one after the other, over and over, feeling the water under the balls of his feet, sending ripples across the waves as fish below look up in awe.

NOT THE SAME

At his funeral they played the Beach Boys.
God only knows what I'd be without you.
God only knows what I'd be without you.
God only knows what I'd be without you.

    He died unexpectedly of a heart attack in the kitchen. You asked me at the wake, cupping a small plate of cocktail shrimp in your hand, Would it have made any difference if it had happened in the living room, the bathroom. You said, It shouldn't have been like this. Like you could see. It's just so fucked up, you said. His body in the coffin, hands folded across his chest but stiff and not really touching. He wasn't wearing his glasses, but on the bridge of his nose were two deep divots—

    You used to say the only good thing about being born is that it was the most traumatic experience you'd ever have, and you didn't remember it. To think, you said, of being forcibly removed from the safest place you'd ever know, of having it turn on you, and realizing that it was ugly and vulnerable and didn't want you. You were glad not to remember it, though there were times when I saw you curled into a ball like string, with piles of blankets arranged around you in a nest, and you were hugging yourself so tight.

You became a believer after climbing a ladder into the sky. Okay, so it was a tree, and what you saw there you haven't said, but I imagine it was something really spectacular. I imagine you stuck your head through the lowest layer of clouds and the dew clung to your hair, and up there with the air so thin, everything seemed to be breathing.

I sometimes imagine your palms. Not your fingers or your wrists, just your palms. How they are flat and shiny. They smell like you've just been outside, and the wet and the wood is in them. The hill of your heel and the little divots where rain pools if you hold your palms up to the sky on a day when it is falling.

I sometimes imagine your palms. Not your bent knees or your locked elbows, just those palms. How you were so sure, for a time, that they had God in them, how the light came off them sometimes, like they were shedding light. But they were run over with blood and chlorine water and when you held them up they were dripping and held nothing.

You curled up in the branches and you saw something there, that night, while the rest of us huddled around the table with the last of the booze. I wish you had come down; Come inside, I said, but you didn't. You, dark bundle of sticks twined together with mourning clothes. And when the fog descended on you, did you see the shapes of angels in it? Did you see him? Was he there? Did he have his glasses on so he could see—

He said, Run! and pointed. Neon spray paint on the blacktop to mark the end zones. We ran and pressed our hands to the backs of the big kids, making them slow and stop. He gave us that power.

She died unexpectedly in the pool and no one knows why. You found her in the deep end face down leaking blood into the water and when you pulled her out, you tried CPR but her lips were wet and fleshy and foreign. At the wake you said nothing and ate nothing; you just looked at your hands and cried. Here is what I wanted to say to you: What did you see. What did you think you could do. Was it supposed to be this way, this time.

You used to say that being born was violent. Then someone died, and he had the biggest and strongest hands of anyone we knew. Then you said, Nothing is ugly. Everything is perfect. You said, Being vulnerable means you can be broken, and if you can be broken you can be fixed. You were strung out like clothesline and your clothespins were in order, and it didn't make sense to me. But then someone died, and your palms trying to jumpstart her lungs couldn't save her, and now you say that being alive is violent.

I try to tell it the way I know it so that I will understand it. You became a convert after sleeping in a tree. Maybe you were drunk, maybe your words were slurred and the blurriness made it so that you didn't picture him dead on the brown linoleum. You went to church after that. You weren't the same after that. You walked around with this light in your body like you were a lantern and sometimes you stood at the living room window and held your hands out to the midnight.

I sometimes imagine your palms and how the rain runs out of them now and how they are empty.

I sometimes imagine the smallness of our palms on the big kids' backs when we played in the street, and how he could hold the football with one hand.

I was angry at you for leaving me. You left me on earth while you climbed a tree up to God. Why didn't you take me with you. You, bright ball of tin foil who put your shiny hands on people's foreheads and brought their spirits in to your palms. I was just as broken when he died. I was just as broken and I didn't get fixed like you did.

You became a believer after climbing into the sky. You must have huddled there with your arms around your knees, floating on your side in the stratosphere with weather balloons sailing past you. You must have had your eyes closed, and it must have been so quiet you could hear the stars speak from millions of years in the past, their voices swelling out across eons, until you were filled with them, and you, from your vantage point in the future, could hear the present playing exactly as it should.

But what about now—

Are you so sure now—

NOT THE SAME

Are you—

OVER AND OVER AND OVER

PHOTOGRAPHS BY KENT QUIRK, MORGAN QUIRK, AND TRACI CHEE

WHEELER STREET PHOTO PRINTS ©

DEAR PENDLETON,

   YOU LOOK OUT OVER CANYONS LIKE THIS, OVER VAST UNFATHOMABLE DISTANCES LIKE THIS, AND YOU BEGIN TO COMPREHEND HOW SMALL YOU REALLY ARE.

   DO YOU BELIEVE IN GOD?

   I IMAGINE THAT JAGGED VALLEYS LIKE THIS ARE THE PLANES OF HIS PALM, AND WITH HIS OTHER HAND HE IS PASSING CLOUDS OVER THE EARTH. COLD SHADOWS AND LIGHT.

          YOUR FRIEND,
          CJ

MIKE PENDLETON

463 DOUGLAS DR. #17

WOODWORD, MI 48625

S-126

DEAR PENDLETON,

   I AM PRETTY SURE YOU MAKE THE ASCENT TO HEAVEN IN A SKI LIFT.

   PEOPLE AND POWER BEING CARRIED INTO THE PEARLIZED CURVE OF THE SKY, OVER THE STONY UNFORGIVING GROUND.

   YES. I AM PRETTY SURE THAT'S HOW IT IS.

          YOUR FRIEND,
            CJ

MIKE PENDLETON

463 DOUGLAS DR. #17

WOODWARD, MI 48625

S-249

WHEELER STREET
PHOTO PRINTS ©

DEAR PENDLETON,

  I WANT CHARLES TO BE IN A PLACE LIKE THIS: WITH CLEAR LAKES AND BLACK FORESTS, A PATCHWORK OF SNOW ON THE FARTHEST PEAKS, AND CLOUDS RISING FROM THE WATER. HE'D LIKE THAT, I THINK.

        YOUR FRIEND,
          CJ

MIKE PENDLETON

463 DOUGLAS DR. #17

WOODWARD, MI 48625

S-113

WHEELER STREET PHOTO PRINTS ©

THURSDAY AUG 13 2009

DEAR PENDLETON,

I WAS HAVING THIS CONVERSATION WITH A WOMAN AT A BUS STOP. "I CAN FEEL ALL THE MINUTES OF MY LIFE JUST SLIPPING AWAY," SHE SAID, "TILL THEY ARE PILED UP LIKE SO MANY PEBBLES AT THE BOTTOM OF A RIVERBED, AND I AM GONE, WASHED THROUGH BY THE VIOLENT WATERS OF TIME."

"THAT'S TERRIBLE," I SAID.

AND SHE: "THERE ARE WORSE THINGS."

      YOUR FRIEND,
        CJ

S-371

MIKE PENDLETON

463 DOUGLAS DR. #17

WOODWARD, MI 48625

I'VE LEFT YOU A TIP BUT I ALSO WANTED TO SAY THANK YOU FOR TELLING ME THAT STORY ABOUT THE ANGELS, AND HOW THEY SAIL SHIPS UPSIDE-DOWN THROUGH THE NIGHT SKY, WATCHING US THROUGH LONG BRASS TELESCOPES, AND HOW WHEN SOMEONE DIES AN ANGEL LEAPS OFF THE DECK INTO THE AIR AND FLIES TO EARTH, AND HE WRAPS UP THEIR SOUL IN HIS ARMS AND LAUNCHES HIMSELF OFF THE GROUND LIKE AN ARROW, OR A BULLET, AND TAKES THEIR SOUL UP INTO THE SKY WITH THE WIND ROARING AROUND THEM.

DEAR PENDLETON,

  I HAVE BEEN THINKING A-
BOUT THE WORSE THINGS. I MET A
MAN TODAY; HIS CLOTHES WERE THREA-
DBARE, BUT HE CARRIED HIMSELF LIKE
A DANCER OR A FIGHTER, READY TO PO-
UNCE. HE TOLD ME HIS KIDS WERE
MY AGE. HE HAD A HUGE AND UNEVEN
SMILE, LIKE A WINTER SUN. HE SAID,
"THEY'RE ALL I HAVE IN THE WORLD."
AND THEN, "I DON'T HEAR FROM THEM
MUCH ANYMORE."

  YOU CAN BE PROUD AND TERRIBLY
SAD AT THE SAME TIME.
        YOUR FRIEND,
           CJ

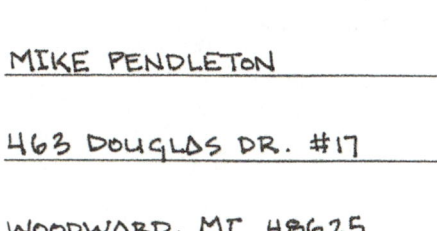

MIKE PENDLETON

463 DOUGLAS DR. #17

WOODWARD, MI 48625

Dear Pendleton,

This is how I want to imagine Charles went. Small and barefoot past the wet rocks and collapsing cliffs into the frothing salivating ocean. On the beach one second and gone the next, swallowed up, with us clambering wildly after him.

Except we weren't clambering, I guess. Maybe not even calling. And when he disappeared around the corner we didn't go after him.

Your friend,
CJ

WHEELER STREET PHOTO PRINTS ©

Mike Pendleton
463 Douglas Dr. #17
Woodward, MI 48625

S-215

WHEELER STREET PHOTO PRINTS ©

DEAR PENDLETON,

THE WORLD IS A LABYRINTH OF ROADS, AND ONCE YOU SET FOOT ON THEM YOU ARE ALREADY LOST, AND YOU HAVE NO CHOICE BUT TO GO CAREENING DOWN THEM, SEARCHING MADLY FOR HOME.

SOMETIMES I FEEL LIKE I'M CASCADING OVER THE EDGE OF THE PLANET, AND I AM BEING DUMPED INTO AIMLESS OPEN SPACE, THROWING WORDS, THESE TENUOUS CONNECTIONS, INTO THE DARK, SO I WILL BE ABLE TO DRAW MYSELF BACK AGAIN.

   YOUR FRIEND,
    CJ

S-176

MIKE PENDLETON

463 DOUGLAS DR. #17

WOODWARD, MI 48625

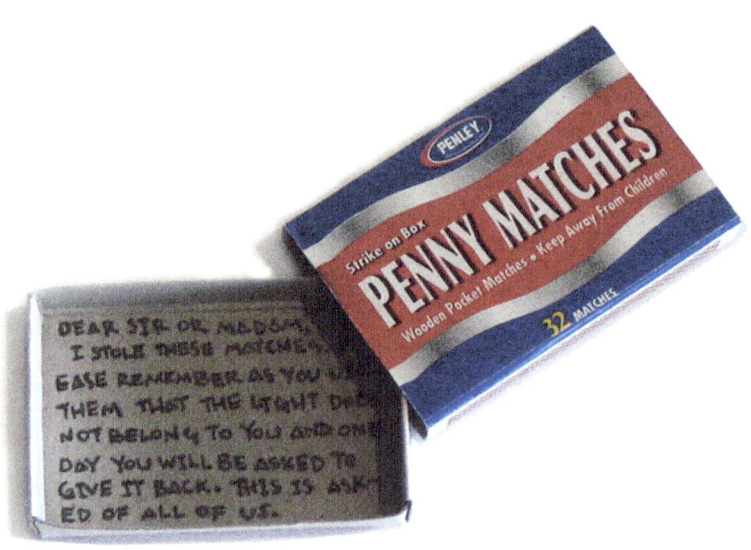

WHEELER STREET
PHOTO PRINTS ©

DEAR PENDLETON,
  PEOPLE ARE REALLY HERE. I KNOW BECAUSE YOU CAN TELL WHEN THEY'RE GONE. DEPRESSIONS IN THE COUCH CUSHIONS. FINGERPRINTS ON A CAR WINDOW. THE WORN-DOWN PLACES IN THE CARPET.
  PEOPLE ARE REALLY HERE... EVEN IF SOMETIMES THEY ARE SAILING ON THE DARK WATER ALONE, BLOTTING OUT STARS, AND THE ONLY SIGNS OF THEIR PRESENCE ARE THEIR SHADOWS, OR THEIR QUIET CURLING WAKES.
             YOUR FRIEND,
                CJ

S-336

MONDAY SEP 23 2009

MIKE PENDLETON
463 DOUGLAS DR. #17
WOODWARD, MI 48625

DEAR PENDLETON,
 I GO OVER IT AGAIN AND AGAIN IN MY HEAD. CHARLES'S MOM CALLING ME, HOW SHE SOBBED. "**IT'S OVER. IT'S OVER. HE'S COLD. HE'S SO COLD. IT'S ALL OVER.**" SHE SHOULDN'T HAVE HAD TO FIND HIM. WE SHOULD HAVE FOUND HIM. WE SHOULD HAVE GONE OVER WHEN HE DIDN'T CALL US BACK. IT SHOULDN'T HAVE BEEN HER. IT SHOULD HAVE BEEN US TO FIND HIM LIKE THAT. GOD. OVER AND OVER AND OVER.
          YOUR FRIEND,
            CJ

MIKE PENDLETON

463 DOUGLAS DR. #17

WOODWARD, MI 48625

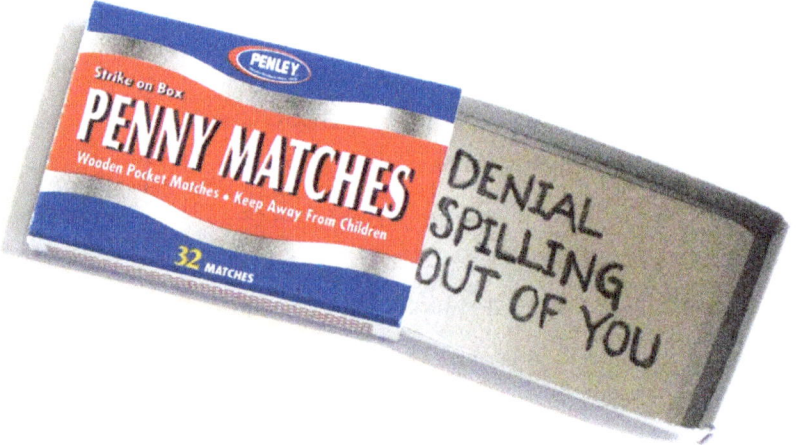

DEAR PENDLETON,

WHY DID HE DO IT?

        YOUR FRIEND,
        CJ

MIKE PENDLETON

463 DOUGLAS DR. #17

WOODWARD, MI 48625

OVER AND OVER AND OVER

DEAR PENDLETON,

  I HAVE WANDERED THE MAZE OF THIS CONTINENT, BACK AND FORTH OVER THE MOUNTAINS, BETWEEN THE SEAS.

  TODAY I SAT ON THE EDGE OF THE PIER, WITH THE SPARKLING HARD WATER STRETCHING OUT BEFORE ME, WITH THE SUN BLINDING ON THE WAVES AND THE BIRDS WHEELING AND CRYING IN THE SKY. I THOUGHT ABOUT HOW I WAS HERE ALONE ON THE VERGE OF ALL THAT OCEAN. I THOUGHT ABOUT DIVING IN AND GOING AND GOING AND GOING UNTIL I COULDN'T ANYMORE.

          YOUR FRIEND,
            CJ

WHEELER STREET PHOTO PRINTS ©

MONDAY NOV 30 2009

MIKE PENDLETON

463 DOUGLAS DR. #17

WOODWARD, MI 48625

S-109

DEAR PENDLETON,

WHY WERE WE ALWAYS SO GODDAMN SERIOUS? THIS IS A CONVERSATION I HEARD TODAY, BY A COUPLE GUYS NOT MUCH YOUNGER THAN US.

"YOU KNOW WHAT THE WORLD NEEDS MORE OF?"

"WHAT?"

"NIPPLE TASSELS."

"YEAH!"

WE NEVER SAID SHIT LIKE THAT. WHY COULDN'T WE JUST BE YOUNG AND STUPID?

YOUR FRIEND,
CJ

MIKE PENDLETON
463 DOUGLAS DR. #17
WOODWARD, MI 48625

Dear Pendleton,

  I think Charles must have felt out of place here on the firm and unmoving earth, feeling daily like he was drying up and turning to dust, and he was parched and stricken by this not belonging. And his failed attempts at camouflage only made him more conspicuously alone.

         Your friend,
            CJ

Mike Pendleton
463 Douglas Dr. #17
Woodward, MI 48625

DEAR PENDLETON,
  DO YOU REMEMBER WHEN CHARLES BROKE THAT GUY'S ARM? THAT GOD-AWFUL CRACKING. I DON'T EVEN REMEMBER WHAT FOR. CHARLES WAS CRYING. I NEVER SAW HIM CRY LIKE THAT, LIKE IT WAS HIS OWN BONES SNAPPING. WE SHOULD HAVE STOPPED HIM. WE COULD HAVE STOPPED HIM. BUT WE DIDN'T.
                    YOUR FRIEND,
                    CJ

MIKE PENDLETON
463 DOUGLAS DR. #17
WOODWARD, MI 48625

WHEELER STREET
PHOTO PRINTS ©

S-314

OVER AND OVER AND OVER

PAPER CUPS AND COFFEE BEANS AND FRENCH ROAST AND HERBAL TEA AND WET JACKETS AND SLIPPERY FLOORS AND WOODEN CHAIRS AND CUSHIONED CHAIRS AND THE JINGLE OF CHANGE IN THE DRAWER AND THE CAR AT THE DRIVE-THRU WINDOW AND THE SCREAM OF THE ESPRESSO MACHINE AND MOPS AND BROOMS AND WINDOWS DRIPPING RAIN.

THERE IS SO MUCH TO THE WORLD, AND THERE IS NOT ENOUGH.

This old lady said to me, "I don't understand why kids these days like to touch each other so much. It must be from the comedies."

I told her sometimes even laughter is an act of desperation. All the pushing, shoving, prodding, kissing, trying to get through to another human being. To prove you're not alone.

She said loneliness is a fragile thing. "You get to my age," she said, "and you hold on to your loneliness, because beyond that is nothing."

Your friend,
CJ

Mike Pendleton
463 Douglas Dr. #17
Woodward, MI 48625

WE HAD THE SAME NAME. I KEEP COMING BACK TO THAT. WE ALL DECIDED TO CALL ME CJ BECAUSE HE WANTED TO BE CHARLES, LIKE CLINGING TO THAT NAME WOULD BE ENOUGH TO KEEP HIM HERE.

SOMETIMES THESE DAYS I FLICK ON AND OFF LIKE A LIGHT SWITCH. SOMETIMES I AM HERE AND SOMETIMES I'M NOT. I SPEND A LOT OF TIME THINKING OF WHAT HE WOULD BE DOING, IF HE WAS THE ONE AIMLESS AND WANDERING, AND I HAD BEEN THE ONE CUTTING MY WRISTS LAST WINTER.

YOUR FRIEND.

MIKE PENDLETON

463 DOUGLAS DR. #17

WOODWARD, MI 48625

I'M NOT YOUR FRIEND. YOU DON'T EVEN KNOW ME. I JUST WANTED TO TELL YOU THAT I WAS HERE. I SAT IN THE BOOTH BY THE CASH REGISTER AND I ASKED YOU IF YOU BELIEVED IN GOD. YOU SAID, SURE I DO. I SAID, I DON'T KNOW IF I CAN. YOU SAID, DON'T KID YOURSELF. YOU CAN BELIEVE ANYTHING IF YOU'RE PUSHED FAR ENOUGH. MY NAME IS CJ. DID YOU KNOW THAT I'M CJ. THE C STANDS FOR CHARLES AND I WAS NEVER A VERY GOOD FRIEND.

SOMETIMES I GET THE FEELING THAT THINGS ARE LEADING UP— NOT LOOKING, JUST LEADING — AND I'M CLIMBING STAIRCASE AFTER STAIRCASE SEARCHING FOR SKY. I'VE BEEN THINKING ABOUT CEILINGS AND HOW THEY'RE LIKE SHACKLES AND HOW THEY MAKE YOU WANT TO GO BURSTING THROUGH THEM, SPLINTERING SUPPORTS AND SHINGLES, LIKE A SUDDEN GIANT. WITH CLOUDS CLINGING TO YOUR HAIR AND HUNDREDS OF COLD AND TINY HANDS TUGGING AT THE LACES OF YOUR SNEAKERS. I'VE GONE ALL THIS WAY AND STILL THE WORLD DOESN'T SEEM LARGE ENOUGH.

YOUR FRIEND.

MIKE PENDLETON

463 DOUGLAS DR. #17

WOODWARD, MI 48625

OVER AND OVER AND OVER

I TRIED TO LEAVE THESE THINGS BEHIND SO THAT I COULD FOLLOW THEM BACK, NO MATTER HOW FAR I WANDERED OR HOW LOST I WAS.

BUT AFTER ALL THIS, HOW CAN I MAKE IT HOME? HOW CAN I POSSIBLY RETURN, WHEN THE WORLD SPINS SO FAST, AND I'M DOING ALL I CAN JUST TO PREVENT MYSELF FROM BEING FLUNG INTO THE COLD DEPTHS OF SPACE? HOW CAN I SLOW DOWN ENOUGH TO COME BACK?

WHEELER STREET
PHOTO PRINTS ©

FRIDAY JUN 25 2010

MIKE PENDLETON

463 DOUGLAS DR. #17

WOODWARD, MI 48625

S-237

WAS THERE A NOTE? THE POLICE CAME BY AND THEY ZIPPED ALL THE LAST IMPORTANT THINGS INTO PLASTIC BAGS AND THEY DIDN'T GIVE ANY OF IT BACK. JUST HIS BODY. FUCK. AT LEAST THEN WE REALLY KNEW IT WAS OVER. EXCEPT IT'S NEVER GOING TO BE OVER, IS IT? I WANTED THERE TO BE A FUCKING NOTE. WHY DIDN'T HE LEAVE US <u>ANYTHING</u>? WE, WHO HAVE TO KEEP GOING WHEN HE'S GONE?

   I LOVE YOU. I MEAN **FOREVER**. THAT'S WHAT I WOULD HAVE SAID, IF I WAS HIM. ADDRESSED TO EVERYBODY. MEANING IT. I WOULD HAVE GIVEN YOU SOMETHING. AND EVEN THEN, THERE WOULD HAVE BEEN SO MANY THINGS I NEVER GOT A CHANCE TO SAY.

MIKE PENDLETON

463 DOUGLAS DR. #17

WOODWARD, MI 48625

DEREK

Imagine the world is a tin can, and our car is a can-opener and we're carving the lid off this motherfucker with every mile. We're going up California, sawing her in half vertically, splitting her down the central valley, heading who knows where, maybe Oregon, maybe Vancouver, maybe back to the U.S. of A. in spitting-cold Alaska.

For now it's enough to be leaving L.A., to watch the Hollywood sign in the passenger's side window appear and disappear behind warm smog-coated rooftops, to know we won't be seeing it again, except maybe on HBO as we sit in a motel room somewhere north of the border.

For now it's enough to know that we won't have to endure this tepid excuse for autumn anymore. We'll go somewhere with *seasons*. With a real fall, with leaves tumbling out of the sky and frost on the grass in the morning. With a real winter, with dirty molehills of slush on the sidewalk. We'll go slidey slidey slidey over the streets but fuck if our tires ever leave the road.

We're over the Grapevine, scaling that stark son of a bitch in the slow lane, windows down, lukewarm So Cal breeze on our cheeks, singing ourselves hoarse and cranking up the radio until we can't hear ourselves screaming—

Then we're coasting down the last crest, watching the 5 meet the 99 on the valley floor in a lambda, and god could we be any closer to rocketing right off the face of the earth? There's autumn sun on the dead grass and white clouds coating the sky like stucco. That open road is just begging for us. We hit the valley running and go and go and go.

*

We're clipping along at 85 miles per hour and the fields spread out around us. Miles and miles of farmland and nothing else. We gaze through the windows and talk about Derek without looking at each other. Remember the crook in his middle finger? From holding a pencil. Yeah, he wrote everything longhand. Only used a keyboard for clerical work. Remember the sunburn? We always said Derek was going to die of melanoma. He would have, if that truck hadn't hit him. He used to spend entire afternoons outside reading. Making the books damp with his sweaty palms. Remember the time he picked us up from that bar because we were too shitfaced to drive? Remember when he used to say, "Jesus Christ, what the fuck are we doing here? What the fuck are we doing?"

After the first eight hours, we're coughing up the remnants of L.A.-yellow air and, having driven for so long, we're developing an intimate yet flagging relationship with our car. She's starting to smell because we're starting to smell—you can only eat so much In-N-Out before your pores begin leaking grease—and goddamn we wish it wasn't pissing rain today because we'd roll down the windows if we could. Just to feel the chill.

We crack a window anyway, get peppered by drops as big as our fingernails. The thighs of our jeans polka-dotted with water. We grin and our ears go numb.

We've stockpiled a set of rolled-up Doritos bags, stuffed them into Icee cups. We plan on discarding them at the next gas station. But we don't. We tell ourselves it'll be the next pit-stop, and the next, and the next, but we forget. We carry our trash with us, leaving no traces of our arrival or departure. We're nomads. Gypsies melting into the horizon. We plan to pitch tents when we get far enough into the wilderness.

*

The rain stops when we plow through Sacramento and kiss it goodbye. We travel through cow country, wet and flooding in the low places. It's been nearly ten hours now, maybe half a day, and the sky is low above us, gray and pressing down. We find a classical station and listen to opera and the occasional puddle under our tires.

We talk about Derek. Remember how he died. He was waiting at a stoplight when a pickup truck clipped the bumper of a speeding SUV, sending it spiraling onto the sidewalk. He was pinned to the lamppost by the grill of a Cadillac. They had to saw the car away from him, but he had already been cut in two.

We went to the funeral. We wore newly dry-cleaned suits. Someone said, "For what is it to die but to stand in the sun and melt into the wind?" We sat in the pews and looked at our fingers.

There was a wake at Derek's parents' house. We attended. We gave John and Annie our condolences. We stuck around for hours, watching the flowers wilt, watching cousins, colleagues, aunts and uncles come and go, filtering in and out of the house like tides. We only spoke when spoken to; otherwise, we stood in the dining room, picked at the hors d'oeuvres and wiped our fingers on the paper tablecloth.

A lady with stooped shoulders and a black shawl approached us. Her shoes creaked. She squinted at us and said, "How did you know Derek?" Her voice creaked too.

We said, "We've known him since elementary school."

We said, "He was our friend."

"I sent him a greeting card and five dollars on all the national holidays," she said, "including Labor Day."

We said, "You must be his great aunt."

We said, "He used to tell us about you."

"He said he wrote back to you."

"He said you were his favorite."

She smiled. We smiled. Funeral smiles, coming out confused and twisted up.

When we finally left, we went to a florist. We bought some flowers and put them by that dented pole. We stood on that street corner with our hands in our pockets, watching traffic speed past us until night fell and it became hard to see the cars. Just the trails of headlights hovering over the asphalt. And we hoped to god Derek was riding a comet across the universe with solar wind in his hair and sunburn on his cheeks.

When it gets dark we stop at a motel. We gather handfuls of candy bar wrappers and empty soda cans and sneak them into the dumpster at the back of the building. We feel crafty.

The room we share has a hole in the bathroom door where the knob used to be. It's stuffed with toilet paper for privacy. We have cable, but no HBO. The beds are limp sponges and the crack in the window lets in a ghost-like draft.

We don't sleep well, and when we sleep we dream about stop signs and car crashes and slick streets. About losing limbs and someone yelling, "Timber!" as we hit the sidewalk.

We wake up the next morning with neck pain and find a quarter-sized spider in the bathtub. We name him Odysseus and set him free on the drain pipe outside. The motel gives us a continental breakfast and we pocket every packet of jam before heading north.

*

We packed our bags one day, but we left most of our shit in our apartments. We paid rent for another month. We closed up our cubicles.

"Where to?" we said.

"Anywhere," we answered.

We spun a pencil on the hood of the car and it pointed us north. We got in, gunned the engine, and left.

When we crossed that intersection, we shut off the radio and tipped our fingers at Derek's corner, but we didn't slow down.

Now we're sucking apricot jam—the only flavor left—out of those little plastic containers and stacking them one on top of the other until we've built replicas of our old office buildings. Are we in Oregon now? We had no idea California extended past Chico—yeah, Humboldt and Eureka, sure, but who knew there were mountains up here? Huge mountains. What are these, the Cascades?

The freeway slides into a narrow double-lane highway, makes us go slow. We open the windows to smell the air sweeping off the snow-capped peaks. It's cold air, yeah, but we're so high up now we're in the fucking sky and only the trees are closer than us.

We stop at a lake. What lake? Any lake, it doesn't matter. We just want to get out of the car for a minute, for an hour, stretch our legs, do some yodeling, do something. We stop at a lake and strip naked and leap in, treading the air seconds before we strike the surface.

Jesus Christ, it's cold! We freeze and our muscles go solid before we remember how to kick our legs, how to pump our arms. We swim to the surface, gasping for air, unable to see anything but bright.

Teeth chattering, clutching our elbows, we high-step out of the lake onto the sandy shore. We wrap ourselves in the towels we stole from that shitty motel and we shiver.

We sit on the shore, silent, watching as every so often a flock of birds flies over us.

The lake slices the world in two at its waist. Every branch of every tree is deep in the water, every crag on every mountain rising over it; all the little animals are sunk, but breathing, pawing at passing trout. We wonder if we're in the lake somewhere too, faces turning blue, staring up at the sky, raising our hands like someone will reach past the surface and grab our pale wrists.

He will haul us out of the water. He will remind us that the world is a whole.

He'll say, "What the fuck are you doing here?"

I'll look at you and grin.

TO KEEP ME AWAKE AND ALIVE

If I could I would say to you: *Love, come find me.* I would say, I'm sometime between the boating accident and my imminent rescue, or death. You'd maybe want to know that to pass time—to keep time—I recite "Jabberwocky." How much time passed? Have I kept any? One-thousand two-hundred and sixty-three Jabberwockies, but that's a guess, really, because it began with the counting and the counting didn't begin at the beginning, that inestimable span of time spent or passed or kept by mulling over my somewhat ambiguous and certainly dark situation before deciding to recite Lewis Carroll: of all things, the only one I could remember or repeat.

It's one thing to be sailing—to be catamaraning—across a sea like a sheet of steel, sharp against the water, with the shine on it and the slithy toves gyring and gimbling in the wabe, and me skimming over it all spiritquick and free.

It's quite another to be capsized, upturned, head-down in the water with the canvas all a-tangle and the rigging and the ropes dangling like chandeliers. Not to mention the wet monster body with a hum like a generator or a fog horn or a big rig on a fast freeway: the barnacles like pimples or pustules but rock-hard and concrete-stuck to skin, the jaws that bite, the mouth with brush-like teeth, and, love, isn't it strange I thought of your hairbrush but instead of strands of copper stuck to it, there was plankton.

Sometimes instead of reciting "Jabberwocky," I sing Peter Gabriel's love ballad, "In Your Eyes," though I don't know why I don't know the words and have never seen *Say Anything*, in fact I'm not a fan of John Cusack at all but I like the way it sounds when I go snicker-snack and the echoes sing back, *in your eyes in your eyes in your eyes*. What it is is true, and I never told you this but if I could I would tell you now that Mr. Gabriel is at his most articulate when he says there's a doorway to a thousand churches in your eyes, the resolution of all the fruitless searches.

I go snicker-snack and I sing but the whole time I'm thinking of you and how you told me not to go you said, 'twas brillig, with the clouds all over and the wind going through and through, you said Clyde that's not good sailing weather, and really you were right, it's just sometimes this emptiness fills my heart. I didn't know how to say it then but I used to want to run away. I used to want to drive off in my car. What I should have done is stayed put, stayed there and said just once, one-thousand two-hundred sixty-six, it would have been nice to be able to say to you just once, without repeating myself, *Love, I get so lost sometimes*.

If I could I would say to you, I'm sorry I'm sorry, though however many times I say it it never seems to stick. Could I have told you that sometimes the world comes unstuck in my hands and every moment keeps slipping away? I'm not trying to be uffish I'm just trying to be honest and I'm somewhere between water birth and extinction and that's either a ways off or around the corner, I couldn't say, but I'm worried I'll be left for dead.

I'm sometime before the heart stops, the great galumphing thing like a subwoofer, before the body goes cold and either sinks to the ocean floor and all the little fishies eat me an escape hatch and the pressure maybe kills me or I rush to the surface and take my first breath of fresh air in a million Jabberwockies and In Your Eyeses, or the body is washed ashore and machetes or vorpal blades hack me an escape hatch and maybe I am worshipped as a sort of god-in-the-whale—Callooh! Callay!—or I am dead already and then my body will be cremated and my ashes will go up in the light the heat...

I want to come to your arms.

Even if I know nothing else, not where I am, only that it's blackest black and I can't see my hand in front of my face, if I have a hand if I have eyes, I know I don't know if I'm here but I know I want to be in the place you are and if somehow you can hear me you will find me between one-thousand two-hundred and sixty-eight and one-thousand two-hundred and sixty-nine, singing.

RAFT

First I will tell you about the water: the pitch and the roll, the slow ascent of the wave and the sudden plunge, the climb and swell before the drop. I will mention the nausea, the gut-churning, bowel-contracting sickness, where your stomach rises to your throat and sits there, a wet knot you can't swallow, but only briefly, because sometimes the sea is calm. Quiet as a blank sheet of paper under the fog. I will tell you about the vastness of the ocean, and how the horizon is an unbroken line blurring into a seamless sky.

The plane was a crumpled ball of metal plummeting out of the blue.

I was scrambling to get out. The cockpit of my little plane was collapsing, lights flashing, with the sounds of reinforced steel snapping, and the whine and the wail of all that machinery shutting down and screaming for help—and then I was out, and the only sound was of the air ripping apart.

My face grew tight in the wind. I took your name out of my pocket. I wanted one last time to say I love you, to hold your name in my palms and whisper to it as though you could hear me—across the world no matter where you were.

But when your name came out it caught the air, billowing above me like a great silk sheet, containing the wind, slowing me down. I came out of the sky and your name was the only thing that saved me.

The water rose up.

Then the water came down.

I held your name to my lips and I blew, and blew, and blew... until your name filled up and became lighter than the ocean. I climbed into it, and your name was my cradle, orange and inflatable. The sky was blue, and so was the water, and there I was, inside your name, floating and praying for rescue.

When we met, it was cold out, and the days were bright and endless. We were at a bus station, and you were sitting with a plastic lunch cooler at your feet. You were eating an orange and the juices spilled over your fingers, sticky and sweet, and you couldn't shake my hand, but you smiled and touched your shoulder to my shoulder.

"Hello." You had freckles on your nose.

"Hello."

"Would you like some of my orange?" You fingers were slender and chapped.

"I would, thank you."

"You know, you look really familiar." You squinted and looked sleepy. "Have we met?"

"We've met now, because of your generosity with oranges."

When you smiled, it soaked across your whole face. "Ah, but what about you? I don't know anything about you."

"How about this: I'm in Alaska because I'm learning how to mush."

"Mush what?"

"Mush dogs." I told you about being a kid, living on a small cattle ranch, having two Australian shepherds named Rocky and Hank. I told you about riding horses over dry hills as the dogs darted over the ground, quick as winks, with an intensity and a joy lighting them up as they ran. I told you about how, back then, I wanted to be a musher, with nothing under my feet but the sledge and the snow, calling, "Gee!" and "Hah!" to an ecstatic pack of dogs, paws beating against the ice, tongues lolling, wind catching in their fur. "But somehow I became a pilot instead," I said, "with a metal bird between myself and the air."

"And you're here now to fulfill your childhood aspirations?" you asked.

"I took a few weeks off to learn."

You pulled a wedge of orange from your half. We listened to the soft ripping sound. "Well," you said, squeezing the slice so that it dripped into your palm, "I'm not here for anything as interesting as that."

"What are you here for?"

"I'm taking pictures of snow."

"Snow."

"Snow."

"White snow?"

"That's right." You grinned.

"Snow on things?"

"No, just snow."

"Why?"

"Because," you said. You licked your fingers and then your palm. Your tongue was pink and soft over your dry skin. "Snow makes everything so quiet. It presses all the sound down beneath it and for some reason when the sound goes away, your vision becomes clearer too."

"So you're hoping to see something in the snow?"

"God."

"Destiny?"

You tilted your head at me. "Sure. Fate. Why not?" You stuck the wedge of orange in your mouth and closed your lips over it. You chewed. I watched your jaw moving. "Christ," you said when you swallowed, "there's just something about you. Why do I feel like I already know you?"

When our bus came, you took out a moist towelette—you always carried them, you said—and rubbed it over each of your cuticles, fastidiously.

I will tell you about the misty cold that settles on me in the predawn, coating my neck and arms, seeping through my clothing. I will tell you about the scorching sun of the afternoon, burning away the clouds, glaring down at me, where I am huddled in a corner of your name, blinded, and nearly deaf too, from all that light.

I will tell you about the night. The sky changes, so it's no longer a blank page but an echoing dark speckled with tiny stars. And I tell you, you've never seen more stars than I'm seeing now. There are more stars here than glistening lights we can see from our rooftop on a clear night. Even if every light in every city for a hundred miles was turned on, and all the windows in all the homes and storefronts and skyscrapers and warehouses, and all the traffic lights turned red and green and yellow at once, even if all the cars on the road and in parking lots and driveways had their brights on, even if every man, woman, and child was holding a flashlight up to the sky, there would not be as many little lights as there are now.

I shiver. It's cold, and I wish you were here with me, with a wide lens and a long exposure, tucked under that woven blanket with the faded rainbow trout on it, with your head on my shoulder and your hands, smelling sour and acidic from stop bath and developer, rough in mine. I wish you were here in wool socks and heavy hiking boots encrusted with mud and sticks of old grass, and your oversized hunting jacket, with the lining worn thin and holes in the innermost pockets. I can even imagine you sighing into my neck and saying, "It almost looks flat, doesn't it? Except I know it's not flat, and if only my sight were strong enough, I'd be able to look out all the way to the edge of the universe."

And when we got back home, you'd spend early mornings looking at huge four-by-three foot prints of blurry, streaky stars, staring at the black spaces between them, trying to see past your range of vision.

Sometimes I turn onto my belly and lean as far as I can go without tipping into the sea. I lie there, looking at the dark water, but the shapes I see are not reflections.

"Hello shapes," I say.

And the water says back to me:

> Hello there.

"Have you been there all along?"

> Yes.

When the water speaks it is not with sound. It is not with language. It is not with images. The water speaks in the cross-hatching of light across its surface, in the black shadows of waves and the sharp edges of reflection. The water speaks with a slow fade into the depths and the shafts of sun reaching down into it.

"I'm sorry," I say. "I've never noticed you before."

The water shrugs.

> That's narcissism
> for you.

"It's not that I'm narcissistic, it's just that I'm distracted."

> That's what Narcissus said
> before he died,
> and left only an Echo behind.

"I'm not going to die."

The water laughs. It's a ripple of shadow beneath the surface.

> Denial
> is not a river
> in Egypt.

I shake my head. "I like you, water, but you're more cynical than I expected."

> I'm not cynical.
> I've just been around long enough
> to know that you can be defiant,

                              but dying nonetheless.

I tell the water, "My love is going to rescue me with a sailboat or a helicopter and when she carries me away I'm going to be laughing."

                    I like you, human,
                 but don't count on it.

I lie here in your name, under night's black blanket, moving up and down with the breathing of the water, listening to it lap and stir all around me. I raise my arms and dip my fingers into the sky. I'm taking the tails of comets and weaving them into a lasso. The rope will be rough and prickly with space debris, but I will knot it with my blistered fingers. I will stand up and swing it over my head and it will make heavy swooping sounds in the cold night air. I will gaze over the curve of the planet, looking for you.

I will see you through the bathroom window, but if you speak I won't be able to hear you. You will be wearing one of my T-shirts and a pair of cotton panties. I will like the look of your legs. The overhead light will reflect off the tile, making you look pale and bright as you perch on the edge of our bathtub.

Your hair will be tied back, but wisps of it will fall over your face and the sides of your neck. You will be wearing glasses. The old comfortable ones, with soft nose pads and flexible temples that bend around the half-circles of your ears. During the day, you wear contacts or chunky plastic frames, but at home you wear these.

The bathroom trash can will be in front of you. You will be cutting your fingernails. I imagine I can hear the sharp snipping sounds as little crescents of nail flick into the trash. You cut your nails short. You always have. You hate the tapping and the clicking, the way it feels when your nail makes contact with a surface before the pad of your finger.

While you clip the nail of your pinky, I will fling the lasso around your waist—a belt of sparkling ice—and I will pull myself to shore. You will drop the nail clippers and run to the window. You will race down the stairs and out into the street, drawn to the beach. Your bare feet will slap on the concrete.

I will pull you to me or I will pull myself to you. When your name scrapes on a shore made of gravel and broken shells, you will be standing with the rope knotted around your waist. You will be breathing heavily, with sweat trickling from your hairline. I will run to you. I will embrace you and wrap us up in light, looping it around our wrists and ankles and I will hold your face delicately in my parched fingers.

*

My hands are in the sky again. I am playing with the moon between my thumb and forefinger. I am squeezing it, squishing it under my fingerprints when the water says:

> What are you doing?

"I'm touching the moon," I explain.

> Stop it.

I turn onto my side and look at the sea, which is black, except for the shards of light on the tips of its swells. "You *love* her," I say.

> I don't.

"You do."

The water pauses—all of its waves go still.

> I do.

"I know."

> Shit.

The water tries to laugh, but it comes out shakily, in a shudder of movement.

> Don't even get me started. I mean,
> I could tell you about the moon
> and that *pull* she has
> and how I never quite make it to the sky
> and how I never rise up enough
> to lift myself off this planet,

even to begin the long journey through the atmosphere.

I sigh, and the water and I sit together silently for a minute, for an hour, or a day, before the water says:

You've been flying?

"Twenty-seven years of it," I say.

To the moon?

The waves clap together, sending droplets of water into the air.

"I'm sorry, I'm not that kind of pilot."

The water reaches up over the side of your name.

Are any of your friends

that kind of pilot?

"No, I'm sorry." I turn onto my back, put my arms behind my head. "I have an idea, though. When my love rescues me, I'm going to talk to NASA. I'll go down to Houston, or wherever it takes. I'll tell them they need to take a container of water up to the moon. How about that? I'll tell them it's more than life and death."

The water trembles.

Would you really?

Would they?

"Don't worry. I'll convince them."

Because there are days or maybe nights when the sky goes entirely black, and the water bucks and kicks beneath me, throwing me into the thick and roiling air like it's trying to dislodge me, and I try to talk to the water, try to ask it to, please, stop, but the water says nothing—maybe because it hears nothing over the shriek and howl of the wind. I will tell you that the rain is a kamikaze, and above, the lightning cracks the sky like an egg, and the clouds obscure the stars, the last splinter of moon. It's because the water misses her that much, and all the depths are reaching out and raging for her.

Sometimes when I'm leaning over the side of your name, thinking of the differences between rafts and bathtubs, the water slaps me in the face. Its hands are cold, body-numbing.

Our bathroom has a claw-footed porcelain tub, chipped, outfitted with a clear plastic shower curtain that's gone streaky and white from hard water buildup. Some mornings, I wake before you, not to see the sun rise or to go jogging along the river, not even to cook you scrambled eggs and spicy, fatty sausage, but to take the first shower—the first shower is always lukewarm at best—so you won't have to.

I reach past the curtain, work the tarnished hot and cold knobs, strip down and wait, naked and goose-bumpy, for the water to warm up, so that when I get in, it doesn't sting with cold.

And when it's warm enough, I part the plastic curtain, and it rustles and crackles under my hands, and I stand there, toeing the chips in the tub, hammered in the chest by cold water.

The water's hands feel like that—except that now, after shampooing and soaping and rinsing myself down, I'm not leaving the bathroom cloudy and steam-filled. I'm not coming back to the bedroom where you're on your stomach sleeping, snoring softly, your back rising and falling underneath the sheets.

The water is just cold and wet, and I say, "What was that for?"

> For almost falling
>
> asleep.

"But I'm tired."

> Well snap out of it.
> You've got to stay awake,
> so you're alive
> when she rescues you.

I yawn. "You said you didn't believe me."

> Maybe I don't.
> But I want to believe in something.

I will tell you about the difference between drinking and drowning, which seem to have a new relevance, lately.

It's a matter of plumbing.

Sometimes I think I see sails on the horizon, white squares of canvas blown by the breeze like book pages, and I think, *It's you!*, but when they come closer, they are only clouds or the misty spouts of whales striking the surface, their long dark backs rising shiny and wet. They're huge. They're mountains moving through the water. I wish you could see them. They have cavernous chests and barnacle-encrusted fins and chins and tails, and when they breach they fly up toward the sky like slow-moving arrows.

They make me feel safe.

But then they submerge again, spraying smoke, disappearing, moaning, into the depths, leaving me only with a desire to follow.

*

I follow you onto the train. We both want a window seat so we settle for sitting across from each other, having our knees and our calves and our ankles touch, so I can watch the scenery as it comes at us, and you can see everything as we leave it behind.

The train goes clackity clackity clackity, but you're quiet that morning. Your face is midwinter pale and you're wearing a multicolored scarf you bought in the Scottish highlands. It's cold in the train car; we both have our coats on still. Our hands shoved deep in our pockets.

You're looking out the window. I try looking out the window too; there are frozen lakes and snow-dusted maple trees, acres of silent white forest, hard-edged cliffsides cut by dynamite. Instead, I see the dirty windowpane and the streams of ice melting diagonally across it as the wind and the forward motion of the train blow them backwards. I think about little upraised rivers snaking across the cold surface of the glass.

I pull my hand from my pocket, and my knuckles catch on the lining. There's a draft.

"What are you doing?" you ask.

I raise my fingers to the dirty windowpane and touch the glass. I trace the rivulets of water and ice with the tip of my index finger. My hand goes numb.

You sit up, touch your fingers to mine. Together, we run our hands over the glass. We slowly palm the entire surface from top to bottom, imagining we can feel the undersides of the ice rivers coursing under our hands. Our skin goes cold.

We stop in a small, deserted station with footprints in the snow and no one to make them. I fold my hand up with yours.

"Don't fall asleep," you say.

"I won't," I say.

> If I were with her,
> if I could soar up to her
> and leave my trenches dry,
> with thirsty fish gasping for breath...

You clasp my hand and smile, but it's a distant smile, and your eyes aren't in it, as if you're drifting away into sleep, or maybe just away.

> I would run my fingers over her.
> I would spill into her craters
> and fill all her valleys.
> I'd cradle her, and
> together,
> we'd be a small blue marble
> hovering tenderly in the darkness.

"That's nice," I say. I'm trying not to forget but my memory is starting to look like stirred glass, with ripples and reflection in it, and sometimes your words break into pieces. I try to grasp them but their fragments dissolve into the waves, and I am left peering over the side of your name, watching as my memory drifts down, out of the light, to be picked out of the cold black water by tiny transparent shrimp.

Stay awake.

Please.

I'm sorry, I tried to stop it, but you just came apart under my fingers.

The train stops—or is it the bus. You pull out a black Bic pen. You write your name on a piece of paper torn out of your pocket calendar. You put the paper to your thigh and write your name and number on Saturday, March 23rd, but the paper is ripped so it looks like this:

urday

rch 23

I know because I have looked at it many times. I have held it open in my hands many times. I have folded it up many times so that the creases are deep and where there are creases the ink has been rubbed away. But I still remember.

I will tell you about how your name saved me when I fell out of the plane. I will tell you about how your name saved me when I fell into the water. I will tell you about the raft. I will tell you about the bathtub.

Sometimes I am naked in the bathtub with my back against the porcelain. It must have been a long day, because my body is aching and exhausted. I'm squinting; the reflection of light off the tile is so bright I am shriveling under it. Where are you? I'm trying to listen for the squeak of the front door or the clatter of frying pans in the kitchen, but I don't hear you. I know you are out there, somewhere, in the next room or the hallway, fixing your hair or fixing a snack or running a feather duster over the blinds. Or maybe you're stopped at an ATM, withdrawing two crisp twenty dollar bills that smell like ink and grease. At a flower stand on the corner of 28th and Market, you're ordering lilies that look like white trumpets. You're walking, listening to the rust-colored leaves crunching under your sneakers, with a smile bathing your face.

I try to raise my head to look, but my head is so heavy. I try to speak, but my throat has gone dry, and I can only whisper, "Are you there?"

Maybe you answer:

Of course I'm here.

But it isn't your voice. Those aren't words you're using, but light and shadow and movement.

I imagine you're here. I imagine you're curled on top of me with your head on my chest. I'm feeling the pressure of your body against mine. I slowly palm your surfaces, the rivulets of water running to your waist, exploring your skin with my fingertips, sweeping them over the fine lines of your body, the indents, the rises, the ridges, imagining I can feel the throb of blood coursing through the underground rivers of your veins—but then you evaporate beneath my hands and I am touching nothing.

The tiles dissolve and dissipate like dust until the sky is blazing overhead and the floor has melted away entirely, leaving behind a vast ocean stretching on and on and on in every direction.

"I'm going to find her." My voice is a thread.

What are you talking about?

I stand, shakily, as the water heaves beneath me.

You're going to fall.

"I'm going to find her," I say. I sit on the edge of the bathtub.

Stop, please.

Don't do this.

I put first one foot over the side of the tub, then the other. The bottoms of my feet are cold and wet.

No,

you're not going to make it.

I stand, and the water tries to hold me up—it trembles beneath me, straining to keep me afloat, to lock its waves in place; it's shuddering, rippling under my feet—but then I am sinking down into it. The tips of my toes, then my arches and heels and ankles.

"I'll make it," I say. "All the way home."

My calves and knees and thighs. The damp seeping into me as I descend into the dark. My waist and belly and chest. Is the water crying? Are those its salty tears running over my arms and shoulders, soaking into my neck?

Sinking, I watch the surface fade from sight. The waves churn. The water is winding up and throwing itself at the sky. Heaving. Readying for the great leap into space.

Soon I am walking along the bottom, kicking up sand, following the upward slope of the ocean floor, coming to a farther shore, where you are waiting.

When I get to you, when I am smiling and emerging from the sea, I will say, "First I will tell you about the water."

LOVE SONGS

I want to love you *impertinently*, like talking back to a sexy fourth-grade teacher while offering her a juicy Red Delicious. Like Don Quixote against a cloud-raising army of sweet-faced sheep. To love you and say so, to stick my tongue in your mouth when we're standing in line at the grocery store I mean bank or DMV.

I want to love you *geometrically*, so I can measure your angles and prove your theorems. The crook of your elbow ninety degrees. Your isoceles legs of equal length. Your front teeth acute on my lip. The pentagon of your body around mine, and towards climax I will spasm in the increasing frequency of the Fibonacci Sequence.

I want to love you *imperfectly*, with fleshy pink blemishes and disfigurations, to fail, sometimes, and fumblingly make it up to you with well-meant but ill-chosen gifts of crock pots and truck loads of lumber. To love you flawfully or awfully, and say selfish things but not mean them, then apologize with my cheek to your belly. I want to bring you milk and double-stuf oreos when you're sick and forget the fabric softener when I do your laundry but please forgive me I'm only human.

I want to love you $cavernously$, in the dark and with the deep fissures of the earth whispering around us. I want to hold you stalac-tight *with all my stalag-might.*

echoing us

To love you miles beneath the surface, to be with you in unaround corners you cannot see past fathomably LARGE s p a c e s . I want to crawl through your

t
u
n
n
e
l
s

on my knees and offer prayers inside your cathedrals. I want to slide into you on my belly, get lost, and never find my way out again.

echoing us

echoing us

your labyrinths

LOVE SONGS

I want to love you *abruptly*.

        Out of the sky like an $_{anvil}$ or a $^{or\ a}_{piano}$ $_{meteor}$, disrupting your life with catastrophic force so that the way you see the world will be forever altered in the way you sometimes feel like a coil or a spring ready for release. How when it r$_{a_{i_{n_s}}}$ you hear the plinkity-plink of ivory keys and little hammers covered in felt striking taut metal strings. And at the rumble of a garbage truck on Wednesday mornings you think of dinosaurs and tar pits and imminent extinction.

                  plinkity-plink
                       plinkity-plink
                plinkity-plink
   plinkity-plink
                                       echoing

  echoing

I want to love you *voraciously* I want to gobble you up like a box of chocolates, nibble on you
                                                                                         plinkity-plink
during intimate moments and suck on you while watching the evening news. I can't get enough
                                             plinkity-plink
of you I'm a glutton growing FAT and BLUBBERY with love for you give me a lock of hair, a rib or
                                                                                                                                                                                          plinkity-plink
two to gnaw when I'm nervous or missing you. I want to devour you drink you in the curl of
                                                                                                                                                                           plinkity-plink
your finger is like orange rind and your twenty-five cent candy dispenser chicklet teeth the salt at
                                                    a cut of your flank   plinkity-plink   plinkity-plink
your jugular give me a wedge of your ankle I just want to ingest you I mean digest you you you
            your licorice veins   plinkity-plink
yum yum yum.

                                                                           the pads of your fingers soft as butter

LOVE SONGS

I want to love you

echoing

yum yum yum

a handful of your vertebrae like skittles   a shot of your tears

plinkity-plink

ravenously.

I want to love you *darkly*.

yum yum yum

plinkity-plink

I'm not paranoid

I want to love you *insatiably*, and I will never have enough no matter how much you give and how much I leach from you. No matter how many times you say you love me that won't be enough to love you *dynamically*. you'll have to reassure me because even if you I'm not paranoid your love will not be I want to love you *aggressively*, with open palms and violent tendencies. I don't doubt enough. To suck it out of you through your mouth, to kiss you so goddamn hard peels of your skin

yum yum yum   yum yum yum   yum yum yum   yum yum yum   yum yum yum   yum yum yum

plinkity-plink   echoing   plinkity-plink   plinkity-plink

I'm not paranoid

I want to love you *unprofessionally*, I'm no whore. your lips balloon up and when you're pressing your fingers gingerly to them I will sneak up behind you and whisper I love the cinnamon spiral of your ear I'm not paranoid you I love you I love you into the nape of your neck where your hair stops growing and where if you're struck hard enough and in just the right way you'll be paralyzed and you will never leave me.

I'm not paranoid

plinkity-plink   plinkity-plink   yum yum yum

I want to love you

I'm not paranoid

cancerously.

I want to love you *cynically*.   I want to love you *methodically*.

yum yum yum   yum yum yum

I want to love you

you *expeditiously* and with efficiency.

yum yum yum

yum yum yum

I'm not paranoid

a scoop of your shoulder

bluntly.

I want to love you *unconsciously*.

yum yum yum

THINGS WILL NEVER WHOLLY KISS YOU

You say, "I don't want this conversation to end."

I say, "I know."

The tide climbs in, gliding over the shoals and scrambling higher and higher up the beach, taking sand and shells with it, wet bits of glass and gravel. The horizon settles over the ocean like a blanket, with dark folds and warm pockets of sunlight in the clouds, and in the wind from the north, we both tremble, though it's not because of the cold. Your shoulder is so close, so solid and *there*, that if we could make the earth tilt just a little...

It does—I slide four inches to my right, listening to the crackle of your jacket as I press my arm against yours. You take my hand, and together we go running toward the waves. We race into the water fully clothed.

The ocean spills over. Churning up sand, erasing footprints.

We're heavy, and the tide tugs us in different directions, and I think about holding on to each other. I think about swimming. Yes. Striking out for open sea. We wouldn't sink when we got tired; we'd take a long nap in the horizon. Cuddle up together.

And when we woke, we'd feel stars on us. I'd feel your arms around me. I'd lean back, laughing softly, looking up. We'd both be naked, having lost our clothes somewhere in the riptide, pressed skin-to-skin in the depthless bed of the ocean, under the sheet of the sky.

You used to hold me like a book. The anthology of my life leafed through in the flutter of my eyelids. You used to run your finger down my spine like you wanted to read me over and over and over.

One time we tried to build a bookcase in the middle of the living room floor. There were boards and screws strewn around us—you and I kneeling in a circle of wood panels and fastening materials.

You tried the website. "Look at this," you said, reading off the computer screen. "'Two people are needed to *assembly* this furniture.'"

I said, "Come here. We can figure this out."

You came. You laid me flat. We pressed our lips and hips together. Our legs and arms opened out into radii. Our torsos became the thrusting center of disconnected shelving.

We sit for so long on the concrete retaining wall that it's dark when we finally stand. I won't look at my watch. I don't want to know how long it lasted.

You walk me to my car. The streetlamps in the parking lot are orange, and everything looks encased in amber. I imagine that among towering baobab trees in Madagascar, bats and mosquitoes are immobilized in mid-air. And in Manhattan all the meters in all the taxicabs have stopped running. And just behind us, the ocean has frozen solid, the breakers caught in perpetual swell.

We're standing at my driver's side door, waiting for someone to say something.

Like, "This was a mistake." And, "I'm sorry. We tried so hard."

Or, "This is a mistake." And, "Don't go."

Or, "Let's go."

I think about driving off with you, leaping into the car, turning the key, and going. No time for full tanks or maps or seatbelts. I think about you reaching over and cradling the back of my neck. I think about leaning across the emergency brake.

I think about the desert, with a strip of highway stretching east-to-west across the flat land, and no cars but ours for miles. I think about running out of gas. Rolling to a stop. We'd try to push together but we wouldn't be strong enough, and there'd be nowhere to go. We'd wander by the roadside, searching for cell phone service, waiting for passersby as the midday heat swarmed over us. We'd be sweaty and surly, sitting but not touching, not speaking and straining for the sound of motors and the gleam of windshield on the unreachable horizon.

Instead I kiss you. I have to.

You take my face in your hands and kiss me so hard my bottom lip aches. You kiss me with tongue and ankles and belly and wrists, with surging blood and stinging veins and one throbbing heart.

I'm crying. I'm dripping wet and my ink is running.

But so are you. Without shame. With fat tears and sniffles and sobs.

We stand here raining on the pavement, but we can't stand here forever. We'd flood the planet with saltwater, and our family and friends would die floating in their homes. The oceans would creep through city streets, up to the highest peaks, until places like McKinley and Everest were mere islands, and their inhabitants would fight viciously for garden space while the dead sank to the bottom of the sea, to be picked apart by three-foot crabs and long, pale eels.

I climb into my car and shut the door on you. I lock everything and watch silently as you walk away.

ANATOMY OF THE HUMAN HEART

Part I
Humming

 There was a crab in the deep marine hollows of Phil Marsh's heart. He had a plum-colored shell and beady eyes and a crooked crab mouth, and he liked the left ventricle best because he liked the feeling of the blood as it was sent oxygenated and flooding back into the rivers of the body. His name was Esophagus, but Phil only ever called him Gus. Like:

"Gus, what the hell are you humming?"

 It was an August morning, and Phil was on the road with the windows down and the radio on. He liked the warm air past his neck and the sound spilling out of the car. He liked the feeling that it was just him and the hills, the cows and the oak trees and the sweltering tail end of summer, and except for the occasional car heading in the opposite direction, it really was. He loved the drive to school, when he could feel as if the movement of the place around him was a current, and the music, the sound of it running.

"Gus," Phil said.

"What?" The crab had a small crumbly voice and his humming was like small stones tumbling over each other.

"What are you humming?"

"Journey."

"I'm trying to listen to the radio."

"You don't want to listen to the radio," said Gus. "You want to listen to Journey."

Gus liked the glimmering depths of the heart, the slick walls and shadows and little lights. He liked to collect things that came in from the left atrium, make piles, and crouch under them, humming happily to himself.

"I don't want to listen to Journey," said Phil. "I want to listen to the radio."

Gus brandished his claws and raised himself onto his back legs. "No you don't!" he cried. Sometimes he got worked up about things.

"Yes, I do!"

"*Just a small town girl!*" Gus shouted. "*Living in a lonely world!*"

"Shut up!"

"*She took the midnight train going a-ny-where!*"

"I'm warning you!"

"*Just a city boy!*" the crab screamed at the top of his tiny lungs. "*Born and raised in south Detroit!*"

Of course, Gus was right, and by the time he hit the second chorus, Phil had shut off the radio and the only sounds were the whisper of his tires, the roar of the wind, and Gus singing inside his chest. Fifteen miles of this one song over and over, and by the time he rolled into the high school parking lot, he was singing too: "*Street-lights, people living just to find emotion, hi-ding somewhere in the niiiiiight...!*" Not so loudly anyone would hear him, just loud enough that his lips moved and if you were standing close, real close, you'd maybe start thinking of midnight trains leaving smoke trails in a star-filled sky, though you wouldn't know why.

Part II
Sergeant Bumpkin

Phil had a best friend. Her name was Laura. She had auburn hair and pale skin and when she was sick or about to cry the tip of her nose turned bright pink. She had big teeth and a big laugh and she and Phil had known each other since elementary school.

"One day," she said, "I'm going to go to the bridge and stand on the edge and look down at the water." Clutching Phil's pillow in her arms, she sat cross-legged on his bed while he lounged in the desk chair with his feet propped on the edge of the mattress. "I'm going to think about swan-diving and cutting through the water and being so damn fast I go straight through the molten center of the earth, and I'm going to turn white-hot and burst through the other side like a bullet." Laura was always saying crazy things like that. "You know, exploding out through the Himalayas or something. Ka-pow!"

"Yeah," said Phil, "but if the fall or the molten center didn't kill you, the lack of atmosphere would."

She sat up straighter. "I wouldn't die. I'd become a satellite, waving down at you from space." Then she sighed and looked out the window, as if she might see herself there, blipping through the sky. "What would kill me is re-entry. Greg says most space debris gets burned up on the way down."

"Who's Greg?" asked Phil.

Huddled beneath a pile of smoky quartz, Gus said, "Sergeant Bumpkin says they've been dating a couple weeks now."

According to Gus, Sergeant Bumpkin was the rabbit living in Laura's heart. He was a big rabbit with brown fur and one white paw and he said that Laura's heart was a warren, like one of those big *Watership Down* rabbit holes with soft soil and well-worn walls. He said that on their first date, Greg took Laura kayaking on a cold blue lake that was so still they could see all the needles of all the trees reflected in the water.

"Oh." Laura shrugged. "Just this guy I've been seeing. He graduated a couple years ago."

"And he's still around?"

"He's saving up to go to college. He wants to go out of state." She glanced out the window again. "One day I'm going out of state too. One day I'm going to get to Nepal and I'm going to stand there, surrounded by the tallest, coldest, most ruthless beings on the planet."

Phil looked out the window too. It was just past sunset; the air was silky blue with moonlight, and the clouds were soft cataracts across the sky. "Here's the thing," he said. "You're not debris."

Part III
Death

Gus had been with Phil since he was ten, when his father died. The funeral had been at the memorial chapel, and he'd sat through it, face wet with tears and snot, enduring the prayers and the eulogies and the seemingly endless line of mourners who clutched his hands and wrapped him up in their embraces.

But at the wake, back at their small house, nobody paid any attention to him. It was as if he had shrunk, become anonymous in his grief, and he could sit beside the dining room table while the grown-ups drifted through the rooms, looking like enormous black fish at the bottom of a murky pool, with waxy faces and hands that didn't rest, fluttering from hip to lapel to pocket and back again.

Phil sat at the end of the table beside an untouched fruit tart. He was fascinated by the crumbling shortbread crust, the glistening gluey custard smelling of sugar and cream, the perfect concentric circles of kiwi and mandarin orange and blueberry arranged in neat little rings that extended like ripples from the strawberry-blackberry center, all of it sparkling with sugar, smelling wet and fresh as rain. It was bright and brilliant and perfect, and Phil sat beside it, hands clenched in his lap, lips pressed tightly together, thinking about its destruction.

He imagined missiles, tiny toy airplane missiles, falling from somewhere near the ceiling fan, loosed by miniature bearded bombardiers with leather caps and flight goggles, missiles whistling down down down and exploding on impact. Yes! He imagined chunks of custard and crust being thrown into the air, tumbling end over end until *splat!* on the tablecloth, the chairs, the Persian rug! He imagined flying shards of fruit dripping pulp and juice, *yes*, slivers of orange and kiwi flung up up then down again! He imagined the thunder of bombs, the ear-drum-bursting crack and rumble, the squelch on impact, the soundless flight of rubble!

"Chuck it!" said a voice.

Poised on the edge of his seat, Phil needed no more encouragement than that to take a moist handful of tart and fling it across the room. It landed square on his great aunt's fat ass and fell oozing to the ground.

"Yes!" said the voice. "Do it again!"

So he did. He ripped apart the crust and the fruit and the custard, squished it between his fingers and lobbed it high into the air. Blueberries went pinging off the china cabinet and skittering along the floor. Blackberries ruined white-collared shirts and silk scarves. Guests had to dig custard out of their ears.

"Yes yes yes!" cried the voice. "Exploding fruit tart!"

No one stopped him. No one said anything at all. They looked at him sadly as specks of tart flew into his hair, onto his face, his shirt, his coat and tie.

It was soundless. Phil sat there, mouth open and teeth bared and eyes squinted nearly shut, with custard on his cuffs and crumbs in his lap, and he didn't cry or laugh or wail. Only his heavy ragged breathing.

Once it was done, he stood, unapologetically, and walked to his room, where he fell face-first onto the bed and drifted off to sleep for fourteen hours while Gus dashed across the floors of his heart, sweeping clutter out of the way with his front claws, making great stacks of pebbles and building blocks, and humming humming always humming.

Part IV
Girlfriends

Phil's first girlfriend was Madison Wainwright. They were in second grade. They chased each other around the playground and shared Oreos. They broke up after a week when she found a PB & J in his lunch. As she explained it:

"I don't like sandwiches and he eats sandwiches."

Irreconcilable differences.

Phil's second girlfriend was Amy Anderson. She was on the basketball team, but so were all the cool seventh grade girls. She liked him because he wore oversized sweatshirts that he let her wear on chilly days. She broke it off after two months.

"It wasn't meant to be," said Gus, tapping Phil lightly on the wall of his heart. "Seventh grade girls don't know what the hell they want."

There was one other, but she wasn't a girlfriend. When Phil was a freshman, the school guidance counselor introduced him to Candice Freemont. She had flawless teeth, and when she smiled she parted her lips just so, like a sliver of moon ripping the night, but she didn't smile often those days. Her mom had just died.

One evening they were sitting on the jungle gym at the elementary school, dangling their legs, with the dusk obscuring the woodchips and discarded sandwich bags below. A low wind roared across the ground, picking up dried leaves and candy wrappers and tufts of hair. Candice said everything looked *apocalyptic*. How it was light but not light, and all the color had burnt out. And you were just waiting for the fire to open the sky and turn you to ash. "When it comes I want to be standing," she said.

"Why?" Phil asked.

"To see better."

"See what? Everything dying?"

Candice turned her head, just her head, to look at him. She had deep-set eyes and the whites glowed eerily in the shadow. "Yeah," she said, and didn't look away.

Phil looked back. "You never told me how your mom died," he said.

"No, I didn't."

"Will you?"

"She killed herself," Candice said flatly. "Took three bottles of pain medication."

"Holy shit," said Gus.

"Holy shit," said Phil.

"Yeah." Her hands were folded in her lap.

"My dad had colon cancer," said Phil, "but that's not the same."

"No it isn't."

Gus thumped one claw on the ventricle wall. "Take her hand," he said. When Phil hesitated, his voice rose. "Take her goddamn hand or I'm gonna pinch you in the aorta!"

Phil grabbed her hand but didn't squeeze. She was crying. The sky was gray and dry and darkening and the wind was curling the clouds in. After five minutes she left.

They didn't speak the next day at school. They never spoke at school. But he came back the next night and the next, always around dusk, to wait for a few hours. On the third night Candice showed up. It was long past sunset and Phil only knew she was there from the rustle of woodchips under her sneakers. He helped her onto the jungle gym and they climbed to the top of the slide.

"When did it happen?" Phil asked.

"A month ago."

"I'm sorry."

"Everyone's sorry," she said.

"I know."

Gus was crouched beneath a jumble of silver dollars. "Go on," he said. "Take her hand. You know you want to."

"I know," Phil said. His fingers twitched.

"Shut up," said Candice.

"I'm sorry."

"Yeah." She took his hand in both of hers and raised it palm outward to her chest. It was dark. She pressed it to her, against the fabric of her sweatshirt. She held it there. It was so dark. His fingertips were trembling, beating lightly against her sternum. She slid her hands up to his wrists, then his arms, his shoulders, and slowly to the sides of his neck. He kept his hand where it was, poised there over her rattling heart.

"C-can I kiss you?" The stutter. The quivering of his fingers. As if matter itself was shivering and threatening to come apart.

"Please," she said.

He dug his fingers into her sweatshirt and pulled her to him. He brought his chest right up to hers and kissed her and kissed her and kissed her until the dark fused them together.

Part V
Vera

Phil liked having Gus as a constant companion. He liked the rustling in his heart, the rhythmic tapping of claws and the tiny bubbles bursting in him like soda fizz. He liked knowing that there was a creature inside him and it was *alive* and it did things outside his control. He liked to think that Gus made him a better person. Like:

"Goddammit, Phil, what the hell are you doing?"

At the kitchen table, crouched over his math book, Phil put his pencil down. "Homework?" he asked.

"Go help your mom with the groceries," Gus snapped.

As the crab spoke, Phil heard the cough and sputter of a car in the driveway. That was a new sound. He quickly stood and went to the side door just in time to see his mom's convertible pull up. "How'd you know she was coming?" he asked.

"I have ears like a bat."

Phil swung open the door. He had long strides and long legs to match and he was leaning over the side pulling out grocery bags before his mom had even killed the engine. "Heya Mom," he said.

She pushed hair out of her face with the back of her hand. "Heya Phil," she said. "Thanks for getting those."

"Sure." He shrugged. "What are sons for?"

She laughed. "Just groceries and gutters, I always say."

Her name was Florence, but she went by Flo, and her car was the only really fancy thing she'd ever owned. It was midnight blue, and as far as convertibles go, it wasn't the greatest, but god, she loved the way it sparkled on the road, and when she drove it she felt fast and young and free. She took care of it on weekends, wore overalls and a tank top and got up to her elbows in grease. She liked cleaning things under the hood, liked tightening things and oiling things down so that when she rolled out of the driveway on Monday morning she could feel effortless down the street.

Phil followed her into the kitchen and began emptying grocery bags.

"Ask her how work was," Gus said.

"How was work?" Phil asked, picking up a tub of cream cheese and a block of butter.

"Same old, same old," Flo said airily. She flipped through the mail, plucking out bills and catalogs. She never ordered anything, but she liked looking and dog-earing and dreaming.

"Harper says it was shitty," Gus added.

Phil wanted to say, "I swear you make this shit up," but instead he grunted in the back of his throat and stuffed a box of macaroni into the pantry cupboard.

According to Gus, Harper was the name of the goldfinch living inside Flo's heart. She was a girl goldfinch, so she didn't have the primary yellow plumage of her male counterparts; instead, she was small and muted, as if she'd been washed out by sun. Gus always said Flo's heart was a little wooden cage and inside it Harper would whistle and the songs would disperse into Flo's bloodstream.

"How was school?" Flo asked.

"Same old, same old," Phil answered. He folded the paper bags and put them in the recycling pile near the door.

"Don't be a jackass," said Gus.

"Don't get cheeky," chided Flo from the living room, separated from the kitchen by a wide tile counter. She slipped out of the pumps she wore to work, left them leaning against each other, and collapsed onto the couch with *Pottery Barn*. She sighed and wiggled her toes in the carpet. "Thank God it's Thursday night, right?"

"Yeah," said Phil. He put the last of the perishables in the refrigerator and sat back down at the table. He stared at his Trig homework but didn't pick up his pencil.

Gus tapped the floor of his heart. "Well?"

"Mom?" said Phil.

"Paisley, paisley, paisley," she said. "Blech."

"Is there something wrong with Vera?"

"What?"

"Vera," said Phil. "She didn't sound so good."

"Oh." Flo turned the page. It made a tearing sound. "She's all right."

Flo bought her car six and a half years ago, once her husband's retirement fund came through. There wasn't much, and they hadn't thought to get life insurance, not in time anyway. But you get to Stage IV. You get two months. It isn't enough time for anything.

So Flo put some of the retirement fund away and bought a used car with the rest. She left Phil with her sister, who was staying with them for a few months, and went to the dealership alone. She sat in the driver's seat for twenty minutes, holding the wheel so tight her hands went numb.

According to Gus, Harper said, "Hon, get the car."

Flo couldn't hear her, but if she had, she would have said, "I can't."

The bird fluttered her striped gray wings. "We need this car," she said.

And Flo would have answered, "I know. God, I know. I know. I know."

And Gus said that Harper started whistling, nothing important really, just something by the Beatles, something simple, something you sing by yourself in a midnight blue convertible in the used car lot with the sun so bright around you that you can barely see. Like:

"*I could be handy... mending a fuse... when your lights have gone...*"

When the salesman returned, Flo was wiping her eyes. "I'll take it," she said. She came home smiling, and her hair was wind-tousled and ugly and she looked breathless and happier than she'd been in months.

"Mom," Phil said. "Mom."

"What?"

"Vera."

Flo shrugged. "She's an old girl, that's all."

"Harper says she needs help with the car this weekend," said Gus. He picked up a stray floppy disk on the floor of Phil's heart and tilted it against another, like a teepee. "And she could use the company."

"Okay," said Phil. He scribbled down the next math problem.

Flo flipped a page in *Pottery Barn* and hummed to herself. "I don't know why I get this catalog," she said. "It's wicker, wicker, all wicker."

Part VI
Demotion

Greg was a nice guy with shoulder-length blonde hair pulled back into a ponytail. He wore plaid shirts and cargo shorts and sandals and on their last date, he told Laura he was going to Colorado to study Geology.

"I've been saving for two whole years," he said. "I start in January."

"I don't want to end up loving you," he said. "It would be too hard."

Phil had to learn this stuff from Gus because when Laura told him, she didn't say much. She was sitting on his bed with a wad of Kleenex in her hand. Her nose was pink. She said, "Some things just don't work out like they should."

Gus said, "Bumpkin got demoted. Now he's just a Corporal."

"What do you mean?" he asked.

"He couldn't tell time," said the crab. "That's always the problem. What the hell is the *future*?"

Laura sighed and fell back onto the mattress. "It was just so *clear*," she said. "Between Greg and me. It was *right*."

"Sometimes you want things," said Phil, "and maybe you're not ready, or the world isn't ready, so you have to do all these other things and wait all this time before you can have them."

"What things?" asked Gus.

"Do what?" asked Laura.

"Go to college," said Phil. "Get a career. Go to France."

"You don't want to go to France," said Gus.

"I don't want to go to France!" Laura pulled a pillow over her face and moaned.

Phil shrugged. "It's just an example."

Gus scratched his chin. "I don't get it."

"That's because you can't tell time either," Phil muttered.

Laura peeked out from beneath the pillow. "What?"

"Nothing."

"One day I'm going to drop out of school and steal Vera and drive until I hit the Arctic Circle!" Laura declared, and buried her face in the pillow again.

"See, Bumpkin and I get *that*," said Gus quickly. "But that's different from a plan, isn't it."

Phil rubbed his cheek. "I guess." He glanced at Laura.

"Fuck my life," she said, and curled up. Phil covered her with a blanket.

"What it is is a *longing*," said the crab. "We know all about *longing*." He paused. "But that doesn't have anything to do with this future thing."

The term for how Laura dated was *hard and fast*. A month into their relationship, she and Greg were standing on top of a mountain. They were sweaty and dusty and their calves and sides ached. But the sun was so bright up there, and the land was laid out before them, unfolding granite ridges and long slopes carpeted with pines. Looking out over it, with the pressure of Greg's hand on her hip, Laura felt so big and so small at the same time. She put her head on his hot shoulder and he drew her closer.

"And then I said I loved him," said Laura. "I mean, how couldn't I?"

"I wouldn't," said Phil.

"I know you wouldn't. You're smarter than me."

"I know you wouldn't," said Gus. He huddled down and crossed his claws in front of his face. "Laura's braver than you."

"I'd climb a mountain," Phil grunted.

"That's not what I mean."

"Climbing the mountain wasn't the stupid thing," said Laura. She drew the blanket over her head and sniffed.

Phil sighed and put his hand on her shoulder. "It wasn't meant to be." He said that a lot. He picked it up from Gus and now he used it for everything. For failed tests and Laura's messed up relationships and inclement weather. For road kill and losing football teams and tardiness. For the dips in the market and misplaced keys and his father's death. "It just wasn't meant to be."

Part VII
Letters

When Candice moved away, she said, "My dad says he can't be in *that house* anymore." She spat out the words. She was twisting the hem of her T-shirt in her fingers. "But that's *our* house," she said. "That's *Mom's* house."

"I'm sorry," said Phil.

Candice squinted at him. "You can only be sorry so much."

He shrugged. "I guess it wasn't meant to be."

"A lot of things aren't meant to be," she said. "But some are." She put her hand to the side of his face.

They spent their last hour together pawing awkwardly beneath his covers. The afternoon was coming in through the window, and when she left, there was sweat glimmering along the edges of their faces.

She wrote him a letter each week for three months. He would get them, slit them open, and skim. Gus would peek out from beneath a collection of blue beach glass or rusty keys or alphabet magnets. "Is that from Candice?" he'd ask.

"Yeah," Phil would say. He'd put the letter down.

"You should write her back."

"I will."

"No you won't."

"I know." Phil would go back to his homework or his book or the TV.

Gus would pinch him angrily. "You're a goddamn coward."

Phil would close his eyes briefly. "I know," he'd say.

Part VIII
Time Travel

It was afternoon and it was raining and Phil was lying on the roof. The air smelled like wet asphalt, that sharp clay-like scent rising off the roads. The sky was patched with clouds, butter yellow in some places and ashy charcoal in others. Every so often another pass of drizzle would sweep across the sky, and Phil would close his eyes to the dusting of raindrops.

Gus was polishing a collection of marbles. "Phil," he said. "Hey Phil."

Phil stuck out his tongue for rain. "What?"

"I want to build a time machine."

"How?"

"I need an instruction manual."

"They don't publish instruction manuals for building time machines."

"Maybe it's in the Library of Congress."

"Nope." Phil tried to be as still as possible. He could almost feel how the trees around him opened up for water.

"How do you know?"

"Time machines don't exist."

"How do you know?"

Phil paused. "Everyone would hear about it if there was a working time machine."

"If I had a time machine I'd keep it a secret."

"Why?" Phil asked. "Isn't that selfish?"

"Hell yeah it's selfish. And safer. You don't want a time machine falling into the wrong hands."

Phil put his hands behind his head. "Where would you go?" he asked.

"You mean *when* would I go."

"Yeah."

"It depends on the nature of time." Sometimes Gus liked to wax philosophical, even if he didn't understand what he was waxing philosophical about. "If the time line is consistent and can never be changed, that's different from a version of time where I can go back and wreak havoc on the past."

"Either," said Phil. "Both."

Gus was quiet for so long that Phil nearly fell asleep. Then, thoughtfully, the crab said, "If I can't change anything, I'd wait to go anywhere until you're an old crotchety man with rheumatoid arthritis and bowel problems."

Phil laughed. "You're talking about the future."

"What's the future?"

"What you just said."

"What did I just say?"

"Being an old man. Waiting."

They both imagined Phil as an old man. He was going to be a lean old guy, one of those men with the loose paper-thin skin but not the gut, not the jowls. He was going to have all his hair still, a thick white shock of it that kind of stood straight up on his head. He'd wear big glasses and use a cane and the orthotics in his shoes would creak when he walked. Neither of them said it, but Phil was going to look a lot like his dad would have looked, if he'd lived.

"Yeah," said Gus. "I'd wait and then go back a day or two before your dad died."

Phil opened his eyes. The day was bright and made him squint. "And then?" he said cautiously.

"I'd talk to Max." Max was the tough briny mussel that lived in Phil's dad's heart, holding on with one big foot while the blood rushed in and out like tides. "And I'd spend a whole twenty-four hours telling him about your entire expansive life. And Max would tell your dad. And he'd still die, but at least he'd know. About things."

Phil felt very quiet. Gus had stopped polishing marbles, and everything inside and outside of him seemed to be very slow. Dirt soaking up drizzle. Grasses bending under rain.

"But if I could change things..." The crab knocked a marble against the wall of Phil's heart, and the clacking echoed through the entire chamber. "I'd go back now, and I'd go back farther, and I'd say, 'Max, tell him to get a goddamn colonoscopy.'"

"Yeah," Phil said quietly.

"Even though that means we wouldn't talk. And I probably wouldn't be a crab."

"But you love being a crab."

"I love being a crab."

Neither of them said anything for a while. They listened to the light sound of rain hitting Phil's cheeks. Gus put the marbles away and sat quietly with his claws crossed.

Phil sat up. He thought about time machines and he thought about his dad. The way he looked in the coffin. How his dad looked collapsed, but not old. Just kind of sunken in, like his skeleton wasn't enough anymore, and what had really filled him out was his laughter, or his indignation, or his rough singing voice, which came out of his mouth with a slight country twang, or the light he got in his eyes when he saw Flo, when he told his friends about Phil. And his body was collapsed and it went into the ground, but he'd never get old. Phil said to himself, "It wasn't meant to be." But of course he didn't believe it.

Part IX
Heart to Heart

There was a time when Harper didn't have a cage, because Flo's heart used to be an aspen tree, and like all aspen trees, it had silvery bark and circular leaves that rustled in the wind, and just before winter, they all flushed bright gold, then fiery red, and fell. Harper used to flit from one dipping branch to another with quick flicks of her wings.

"He can't talk yet," she said.

"I know!" said Max. He wiggled his cilia. "But it's exciting! You never know what he might be." The mussel paused. "What if he's a giraffe?"

Harper fluttered to another branch. "He'll be what he's meant to be," she said. Her voice was calm, but Max knew she was as wound up as he was.

"He could be a piece of pyrite!"

Harper let out a shrill whistle. "Oh, don't say that! I don't want him to be inanimate!"

"Nadine's heart is a toaster and inside it is a slice of bread named Harriet," said Max. "You never know. He might be a replica of the statue of David!"

"Max!"

"That wouldn't be so bad, would it?" he asked. "He could be great art."

"He could be a she," Harper countered, swooping to the top of the tree. "She could be the statue of Nike."

Max blew a jet of water from his shell. "Headless and armless?" he said skeptically.

The goldfinch spread her wings, displaying her flight pinions. "Winged victory."

"A flier? I don't think so."

Harper ruffled her feathers. "And why not?"

"I don't know. It's just a feeling."

"He's just as likely to be an avian as a fish," she clucked.

"I'm not a fish!" cried Max.

Harper laughed. Her laugh was a song. Something shiny and quick. Something with brass in it. "I didn't say you were!"

"You called him a he."

"I know."

Then, when Phil's dad was in bed, when he was bald and half-gone already with chemo and radiation therapy, and the smell in the room was sick and close and it clung to you even when you'd left, the last thing Max said to her was: "I hope he causes Phil all sorts of trouble."

And when Phil's dad died, all the leaves on Harper's tree went from green to brown. They dropped. The branches bent inward. They twisted together. They stayed that way.

Part X
Vitamins

It was early November, and the nights were growing icy and black. Normally, Laura would insist on walking home, but in the winter it grew cold and dark enough that she let Phil drive her. He pulled to the curb and they sat with the engine running, watching the shivering bushes in Laura's front yard.

She jammed her hat on her head and gathered her backpack into her lap, but she didn't reach for the door handle. "One day I'm going to run away and join a nunnery," she said to the windshield.

Settled into a shadowy corner of Phil's heart, Gus was picking at the wrinkles and folds of a walnut shell, but he stopped to explain: "Corporal Bumpkin says Nadine and Fred have been fighting again. Laura thinks Fred's going to leave them this time."

"That's not a bad idea," said Phil. "I'll go with you."

"Typical," Gus snorted.

"You can't join a nunnery."

"A convent, then."

"You mean a priory?"

"Yeah, that."

The crab blew a series of angry bubbles. "*Hell* no."

Laura laughed, but not really. She looked out the window. Her fingers kneaded the straps of the backpack. "I get it from Mom, you know. She says the women in our family fall so hard."

"That's because Harriet is a piece of toast," said Gus. "It's part of her nature to want to be warm and buttered up. It's just that she gets burned so quickly too."

"Sometimes I wish I was more like you." Laura sniffed. Her nose was pink. "Stoic."

"I'm not stoic," Phil said.

Gus rolled his eyes.

"Maybe you're just smart. Relationships are doomed to failure."

The crab gently touched Phil on the wall of his heart, and Phil said, carefully, "I don't think so." He watched the leaves tremble in the cold. "My parents... If my dad hadn't..."

Laura took his hand in hers and smiled, sadly.

Gus looked up. He waited for a moment, then said, "Well?"

Phil swallowed. His voice seemed scratchy, dry, like he hadn't used it in years. "Dad used to do this thing," he said. "You know those pill boxes, the ones with a separate compartment for each day of the week? On Sundays, he'd sit there at the kitchen table—it's funny, I can picture the exact way the light came in, sort of yellow and blue and white at the same time, and I can see him crouched there with, like, a cup of coffee and an empty plate or something—and he'd be opening up all of Mom's vitamin bottles and spilling them into his palm. There were these ones that looked just like Hot Tamales... I don't know what they were for. And he'd take them carefully between his thumb and forefinger and put them one-by-one into each compartment, until Mom had a whole week's worth of vitamins ready for her. And he'd close all the doors with these little snapping sounds..."

He paused. Inside his heart, Gus set down the walnut shell. He was so quiet, so unusually quiet.

"He did that every week, you know? Every single week. I mean. It's just a little thing, but..."

"Come on," Gus whispered. "Come on."

Phil chewed the inside of his cheek before speaking again. "But, like... When Dad got sick... Mom sat at the kitchen table for seven Sundays. Just seven more weeks. And, like, every one of those weeks she took out Dad's pill box. And she'd open all his prescription bottles. And she'd fill the compartments one by one..."

He realized his hand was still in Laura's, and she was looking at him like she was looking over the brink of a chasm or a canyon and she was thinking about attempting the wild impossible leap across. She said, "Thanks." Her eyes were shiny.

"For what?"

"You never talk about your dad."

Phil jerked his hand away. He rubbed the steering wheel.

"No!" Gus shouted. "No, no, no!"

"What?" Phil said. "Sure I do."

Gus flung himself violently against the wall of Phil's heart. He hit it hard and came down flat on his back. "God-fucking-dammit, Phil!" he cried. His six legs flailing.

Phil winced. "It's going to be all right for you and your mom," he said lamely, rubbing his sternum.

Laura shrugged. "Yeah, I guess." She shoved open the door and frigid air spilled into the car. She didn't turn around when she thanked him for the ride.

"No problem."

She slammed the door and walked into the house. Phil started to drive away. And Gus was plucking viciously, helplessly, at the air with his claws. "Fuck! Fuck! Fuck!"

Part XI
Gus

The next morning, there was frost on the lawns and the slanted rooftops. Steam rose from the stiff blades of grass, the shingles, and the wet slats of wooden fences. The bare trees displayed all their gnarled branches and old knotted wounds, but the sun through them was turning the air into silver and gold. It was a quiet morning where you could see your breath, and when you exhaled you blew curling clouds of smoke.

Flo left for work before Phil woke up. She hopped in the car, gunned the engine, and music burst from the speakers. It went spinning out the windows. It was Queen, and Freddie Mercury's voice spiraled up through the mist and over the cold roads, while inside Flo's heart, Harper sang softly along.

"*I just gotta get out of this prison cell. Someday I'm gonna be free—LORD...! Find me somebody to love. Find me somebody to love. Find me somebody to love. Find me somebody to love love love...!*"

When Vera hit the highway the sound dissolved, leaving behind a wake, or a memory you could still hear, faintly, between your lips.

Inside Phil's chest, Gus stirred. He stretched his six legs and his two claws and he lifted himself onto his feet, humming. He walked softly across the floor of Phil's heart, picking up stray objects and setting them into careful piles: buttons and bottle caps, mistakes and stutters and miscommunications. He spent a minute examining the milky light through a smooth shard of beach glass. He put it on his back and trundled around in the left ventricle, stacking the things in Phil's heart.

When he was done, he settled down near a few stray spools of memory, sighed, and unraveled one between his claws.

Two months after Candice stopped writing, Laura took Phil's face with both of her frigid hands and kissed him. It was the middle of the afternoon, and they had just walked to his house from school. His cheeks had been tight with cold. They went to his room and threw their backpacks on the floor and he was just about to ask her if she wanted anything to drink when she kissed him.

He didn't remember how her lips felt or what their tongues did, but he remembered that her sweater was soft under his fingertips, so soft that his hangnails caught in it. And instead of doing homework that day, they lay on his bed, and Laura let him put his head on her chest, where he could hear Lieutenant Bumpkin rustling around in the den of her heart.

Gus rolled up the thread again. He wound it carefully around the little wooden spool and replaced it in the pile with the others. Then he took the piece of glass off his back and held it in one claw. He thought about sand, and tides. He tried to remember Max. Harper had told him about the mussel, his purple-and-blue shell, how in places it was flaky and black. She'd said that he liked movement, and that that was kind of ironic. He was always talking about the way that water swirled or funneled or burst forth, about how it could change things, the movement of it, and sometimes they changed slowly, but sometimes the change came quick and hard and terrible.

"*Each morning I get up, I die a little*," Gus said quietly. He looked up. He wanted Phil to open his eyes. "*Can't barely stand on my feet...*"

Phil yawned. "Gus," he said, squeezing his eyes shut. "What the hell."

The crab poked him in the ventricle with a very pointy toe. "*Take a look in the mirror and cry!*" he said. He flung the beach glass across the chamber and it fell tinkling to the floor.

Phil buried his head under the covers. "Stop it."

"*Lord, what're you doing to me?*" Gus stomped on the floor of Phil's heart. Again. To the beat. "*I spent all my years believing in you, but I just can't get no relief!*"

"It's too early for Queen."

"It's never too early for Queen!" Gus shouted, jumping up and down. "*Somebody!*" he cried. "*Ooh, somebody! Can a-ny-bo-dy find me somebody to love!*"

Finally, Phil opened his eyes and the cold sunlight washed over him. Gus rounded on the second verse, his voice growing louder and louder, disturbing the stillness. Phil watched the mist rising, but he didn't get up.

"*He works hard!*" Gus cried. "*Every day! I try and I try and I try!*" In the damp and echoing caverns, he pummeled the walls of Phil's heart with both claws, shaking his hard-shelled body back and forth, shouting at the top of his little lungs, doing all he could, with the power of his voice and the pounding of his feet, to make Phil move.

I HOPE YOU READ THIS / I HOPE YOU UNDERSTAND IT

pg. 1534 **wish** (wɪʃ)

***n.* 1.** an articulated longing, jointed and reaching out from the heart like fingers, at fountains, birthday candles, or broken bones

2. an ache which may or may not be infused with hope, but which is always unrequited and/or with an uncertain outcome at the moment of being made

3. a desire which requires distance from the present and which stretches across the future, the past, or some remote spatial location

If I was walking the red desert with the red sand crackling under my feet and the heat coming up through the soles of my shoes, then I would be thinking of you and tumbleweeds. You, uprooted forever and wandering the earth looking for home. I would be thinking of you and gila monsters. You, looking ancient and alien and out of place, and I, knowing that you didn't belong here, and weren't here, not really, though I wish you were. Here, I mean.

see also: wells, April 28, Thanksgiving, alien, distance, regret, desire, you, desert, me pg. 34 **alien** (ˈeɪlɪən)

***adj.* 1.** belonging **a** : somewhere else or **b** : to someone else or **c** : of something else; strange, foreign

2. not belonging at all, anywhere

It was how you looked at things, not the look in your eyes but the attention toward the world like it was alien to you, and however far you traveled and however many places you lived or people you loved, holding them would never be anything more than picking up a red stone in a blue world and having the color be nothing to you beyond the acknowledgment that in your hands it was solid and did not belong there.

see also: foreign, stone, home, you, travel, Palm Springs, Mars, Earth, regret, nothing, love, me

pg. 1130 **regret** (rɪˈgrɛt)

***vt.* 1. a** : to have something exist, once, but not anymore, and then **b** : to grieve for its nonexistence, maybe even for its death, and **c** : to imagine the alternate reality where such a thing still exists, maybe even thrives, where you don't carry the desire to change the past in your belly like a stone

I counted to six and every number corresponded to a star tumbling out of the dark and dying, and for each one I made a wish, and they went like this: 1) I should have rolled with you across the fairway and, 2) I should have held your hand more often so that, 3) when you left I would not have knotted my heart into a fist and, 4) I should have regretted you leaving more than I did, so then, 5) when you came back with an alien language on your tongue I would have pressed you to the couch and set together our lips and maybe, 6) I would not wish now to rend time and insert myself into its seams and change things so that I knew then that I would love you now, still.

see also: exist, first, wish, Mandarin, many-worlds interpretation, time, golf, grief, swallow, me, love pg. 510 **first love** (fɛrst lʌv)

***n*. 1.** the person you loved before you grew up and, maybe, because of whom you had to grow up

***adj*. 1.** being too young and too unaware to understand falling in love and yet being able to do so
2. not comprehending what you felt and who you were and what was going on between the two of you until years, even decades later, with retrospect and regret on your side

It's not until now that I can think of dodging through sprinklers with you, over the green at midnight, with your voice still shrill, not like it is now, while you're sailing on a yellow river in another country, watching a duck herder with a cane and a cell phone. Not being able to think of you without thinking of me, who I was and who I became. I wish I had known that it would be you that remained in my blood and my body in a way that I can't escape or ignore. And I loved you first, though I'd kissed boys before you and have kissed them since, and whatever happens next you'll have the biggest piece of my heart because I tore it off and gave it to you before I knew that I wouldn't always have more to give.

see also: childhood, golf, China, Ping, decades, kiss, me, here, paper, heart, you

pg. 631 **here** (hɪə(r))

***adv*. 1.** where I am and you are not

I could have followed you there, but I am not sure if you would have retreated into the Himalayas with a Sherpa and a tree branch to sweep away your tracks, and I am not sure that even if one day you return, you will search me out, though it would be easy because my phone number is the same as it was ten years ago, and it will be the same ten years from now, and I know you will probably not call, but I promise to be here, just in case.

see also: you, escape, Himalayas, distance, there, search, phone number, decade, call, me pg. 398 **distance** (ˈdɪstəns)

n. 1. the space or time stretching between the here and now and **a** : what has been or **b** : what will be or **c** : what you wish for or **d** : what you regret doing or **e** : some other place in space or time or possibility that you cannot get to, no matter how you try

2. what separates me from you, now, always, even when you're standing right here, and you're so damn close I could reach out and press my finger to your cheek, though I won't or I can't and though I wish I could I never will

If time is made of taffy, and it stretches between now and then until the distance between gets so thin that it finally breaks, is it possible for me to compress it again between my palms, sticky between my fingers, until I can get back to you? Until we are just two eleven-year-olds building a tree house together, or you are building it and I am watching you drive nails into the boards from below, and could I close that distance too; could I climb the live oak and hold the two-by-fours together? Could we fasten things so that years later they would not fall apart?

see also: here, now, then, time, tree house, you, saltwater, home, me, fastening, close

THE WISHING FISH

It was one of those days when what you really need is the cold mountain air coming off a lake of snow melt. A day when you need to be spindly and young, light and ready to jump. When you need to have the breath punched out of you when you hit the water. When your teeth need to chatter. When you need water droplets evaporating off your body while you sit on a rock and look down at the sand and gravel clinging to your toes. When what you really want is to be lazy and dreamy, lying side-by-side on a sun-warmed boulder under a hot August sky.

Night settles in at ten o'clock. Our backyard is alive with wind, rustling the coin-shaped leaves on the trees that edge our property, churning the day's heavy air, cooling it, while the crickets and frogs trill somewhere out in the darkness. I zip Rachel and Marie halfway into their sleeping bags, green and patterned with big red lady bugs, before lying down between them on the air mattress. There's a second of silence in which we all look up into the star-speckled sky.

Then: "I don't see any, Mom." Rachel squirms up against my side so she can put her head under my arm.

"We haven't even been out here five minutes."

Marie, on my other side, tugs at my nightshirt and says in that soft gravelly voice of hers, "I want to see one."

"You will, honey."

She's only six, elbowing me in the stomach and knocking her heels against my shins. "Tell us a story," she says.

"A story, huh?"

"Yeah!" Rachel nods, knocking the back of her head against my shoulder.

I stare up at the sky, through the lens of the atmosphere, deep into the black of outer space, where it is cold and quiet and lonely. They say it takes so long for starlight to travel to us that when we look up, we're looking millions of years into the past, and most of the stars we see are already gone—and I can't help but wonder if someone millions of years in the future is looking down on us now, here, beneath the spiny leaves of our oak tree.

"A long time ago," I say, "when the whole earth was covered in water, whenever shooting stars went through the sky, they didn't burn all the way up like they do now. The world was too cold for that, so they fell right into that never-ending ocean. And there was a fish who collected them."

"A fish?" Rachel asks.

"Yes, a fish," I answer. "He would peek out of the water so he could see where the shooting stars fell."

Marie cranes her neck to look up at me. "Why did he do that?"

"It was so dark where he lived at the bottom of the ocean," I answer, "and there's nothing better or brighter for lighting dark places than a shooting star."

"What about a flashlight?" Rachel asks.

"Fish don't have flashlights."

"Oh."

"So the fish would gather the stars in his front fins and carry them close to his chest, through the dark water to his cave, where he stashed them away, and down there at the bottom of the sea, there was this great white light coming up through the roof of his home."

"Pretty," Marie says.

"It was," I say. "But one day, the sun grew hotter and hotter, until part of the ocean dried up and the first island was formed. And that night, a star fell right onto the sandy beach, all twinkly and bright, but the fish couldn't get to it."

"Because he was a fish!" Rachel bounces and Marie and I bob up and down on the air mattress too.

"That's right. He stayed there all night looking at the star, but he couldn't reach it."

"And then what happened?"

"The sun got hotter and hotter..."

"Like today?"

I nod. "Like today. And the earth got drier and drier, and there were more and more stars speckling the landscape that the fish couldn't get to, and he would sit there in the water, looking at the shore, and there were so many stars that the whole land was lit up like a city. And then, the earth got so hot that the stars started burning up before they touched the ground."

"But what happened to the fish?" Marie asks. She sounds worried, as if the fish is really out there somewhere, waiting in the water, watching as the stars burn out.

"Oh, he's around. Every so often, one of those old stars gets knocked into a stream and it goes tumbling all the way down the riverbed to the ocean, and the fish is there waiting to bring it back to his home at the bottom of the sea."

"He didn't find a way to get on land?" she asks.

Before I can answer, Rachel screams, "There's one!" She's suddenly elastic and springy and kicking me. And then:

"I saw it too!" Marie is squeaking. "Rachie, I saw it too!"

They're laughing, and the stars are multiplying before my eyes, a thousand of them appearing and skipping about, bright points of light. I raise my hands and so do the girls. The stars shift under our fingers like sand.

The girls stuff their hands back into the sleeping bags and pull them up to their chins, giggling.

I keep one hand up, feeling Deneb pulse beneath my finger, a little throbbing heartbeat just there.

"Mommy, what are you pointing at?"

"Nothing, sweetie."

I let my hand fall to my side again, but the star's little heart has been imprinted there already, and it drums softly against my skin. I feel like I'm holding something very precious on the tip of my finger, something that might be blown away at the next breath.

When I was eleven, my mom, who was a Den Mother in the local Cub Scout Pack, used to take me along when the boys went camping. Me, the only girl, with twelve boys, a Cubmaster, and a couple other parents. I followed trails through wet fields of grass, where the mud sucked onto my hiking boots and squelched as I tromped through it. I picked my way down rocky hills where my only guides were eerie three-stone cairns made of river-tumbled granite.

But I wasn't alone. I was accompanied by the most beautiful boy I had ever known. He had light eyes—I can't remember if they were blue or gray or green, but they were light—and curly hair, and he wore his Class B uniform tucked into the waistband of his shorts. He was strong, and so was I, and we led the rest of the group to the campsite at Lake Margaret, nestled in the glacier-carved California mountains.

We never got lost. He was perfect, we both were, with tough limbs and resistance to pain. Because he was just like me, except smarter and faster and better at climbing things.

"What did you wish for, Rachie?"

"I can't tell you. Otherwise it won't come true."

"What did you wish for, Mommy?"

I tuck my chin so I can smell the faint scent of no-tears shampoo in Marie's hair. "It's a secret," I say, though really I've wished for nothing. I'd forgotten to make a wish at all.

"I wished for a pony!" Marie declares.

Rachel laughs gleefully. "Now you've done it! You're never getting a pony now."

"Neither of you are getting a pony," I interject.

"Aw, shoot." Rachel says it in a way that she won't in a few years, when she learns words like *shit* and *goddammit*, and says them viciously and without thought. I want to tell her to remember being like this—young and light and feathery under a night breeze—because it's tiny and important and once she gets to a certain age, she won't have it anymore.

That afternoon, even before the last of the group had gotten to the campsite, he and I dove into the cold, bowl-shaped lake and backstroked to the granite boulders jutting out of the water. Silently, we crouched there in the sun, with the wind bellowing down the mountain. I remember the freckles on his back, remember thinking how it looked like he'd been spattered with tiny flecks of paint. I remember his hairless arms, how they were slender, the arms of a boy and not a man. I remember that when his hair was wet, he had a head of gleaming, sculpted curls, and the longer we sat on that rock, the lighter and more tousled his hair became.

We convinced the other kids to jump in the water and left them on the boulders, shivering, while we swam to shore and toweled ourselves dry. We ate salty chunks of salami and mozzarella sticks for lunch, sharing a bag of trail mix for dessert. We bravely scaled the mountain that overlooked the lake, crawling up among the rocks, scraping our knuckles and knees on the granite, and when we clambered to the top, we sat there breathless, watching the other kids scrambling after us. Then, after descending from the peak, we built the fire. We gathered big stones and rolled them into a ring. I hauled cedar logs that left dark spots of sap on the insides of my arms while he collected kindling. He looked at me shyly from under the brim of his hat, smiled, and struck a match.

"Six, seven, eight!" Rachel shouts, pointing.

I look up to the pen streaks of lingering stars slashing through Hercules.

"I'm never gonna have to eat tomatoes again!" she laughs.

"That's what you think," I say.

"Aw, shoot."

"I wish I was a mermaid," Marie says quietly.

"It's a good thing you said it." Rachel props herself up on her elbow and leans over on my chest. "Otherwise you'd have to live in the ocean, and you wouldn't be able to stay with us at home."

"Oh good!" Marie snuggles down into her sleeping bag.

"Hey, Mom." Rachel plops back into the crook of my arm. "Where's Dad?"

I glance toward the house, through the sliding glass door at the blue light from the TV. "He's just tired," I say. Pause. "And he has so many wishes already."

"What do you mean?" she asks. She's old enough not to take my word for it anymore.

"Well, he's got your wishes, and Marie's, and mine. He's got all of us to take care of now. So if he makes any more wishes of his own, he'll be an old, old man by the time they've all come true."

"Daddy's not old," Marie says.

We were sitting around the campfire and the heat was on our faces and the soles of our boots. We sang songs I've almost forgotten now, except for the wisps of melodies that I sometimes find myself singing while washing dishes or checking melons for ripeness, until I notice, and then the songs slip out of my grasp before I can remember them.

The Cubmaster, wiping his hands on his pants and coming from the kitchen area, brandished a plastic jug and a water filter. "Someone needs to go pump water," he said, looking meaningfully at the scouts.

There was a clamor of "Not it!" and "Nose goes!" before the boy stood, and his legs in the firelight were orange and smooth. I stood too—I wasn't going to make him do it alone—and he looked at me across the column of smoke rising from the campfire we'd built together.

We walked down to the water, our boots sliding on the slippery, gravel-strewn stone, and he dropped one end of the filter into the lake. It made a plopping sound like a fish jumping, and for a moment I looked up, thinking one had.

He was kneeling, with the lake making lap lap lap sounds against the shore and his arms making the pumping motion to send water into the jug. Maybe, then, I might have seen the man he would become—it was there in the curve of his neck and the quick way he breathed. He would be running marathons, and his legs would glisten in the sunlight as heat waves rose from the asphalt behind him. He'd be pedaling a single-speed bicycle over a cobblestone street in Nîmes, braking in front of a café serving espresso in transparent glasses, whispering into a young woman's wind-blown hair, *Il n'est rien de réel que des rêves et l'amour.* He'd be covered in trail dust, with the Rockies waking all around him—mountain peaks blushing as the sun caressed them, a cacophony of birds twittering, flitting from one branch to another, the rush and tumble of water in a creek bed miles away—riding a gray mare, looking ghostlike in an early Montana morning. He'd have a pair of strong boys—freckly and brown with sun—leaping from the prow of a motorboat in the middle of a glassy lake, sending sparkling showers of water into the summer air as they dove, and later, he'd be ordering whiskey neat at a well-polished bar and tucking his wife under his arm, while their sons slept in bunk beds back home, watched by his sister or some neighbor who would slip out with a smile when they came home, when they undressed and slid between the sheets, her palm on his chest, his cheek to the top of her head, resting that way, all night.

What I couldn't see is that he would leave me in a year, maybe less, his family uprooted again, to some place like Vermont or North Carolina, and he would never come back.

The fingernail of the moon was on the brink of setting, and when it sank below the horizon, it left the sky peppery with stars. I've never seen more stars than that. I've never seen them so bright or so close, like I could dip one of those silver camping spoons into the sky and scoop up a spoonful. Millions of them multiplying, shedding, until their dust was on our shoulders, just us on the shore with the fire behind us, crouched beside little Lake Margaret in the middle of the Sierra Nevada.

*

I want to wrap up that night, tie a ribbon around it, and present it to my daughters at their next birthdays. I want to make flawless creases along the silhouettes of the mountains so that when Rachel and Marie open it, they will see that it could not have been more perfect than it was.

The question mark of Scorpius emerges in the south. Marie is snoring softly. I slip out from under the sleeping bags. I open the sliding glass door with a rushing sound and sneak into the den. Rob is asleep in the Lay-Z-Boy, his mouth slightly ajar and the bridge of his nose edged in blue light. There are shadows in the ripples of his clothing. I disengage his fingers from the remote control and shut off the TV. It winks out.

I stroke the line of his jaw with my middle and ring fingers. He has long lashes and they sweep upward as he opens his eyes. The girls have those lashes, those eyes. He smiles, and I crawl into his lap and the recliner sways under my added weight. Rob holds me at the ribcage with both of his hands and sighs into my hair.

I put my mouth on his. Thrust my chin forward, push. I want to kiss roughly and quickly so my teeth scrape on his. So it hurts. So it's deep. Like we're swallowing each others' tongues. His fingers climb up my back.

When we part, our lips are moist and our hands are tight on each other.

If the girls were still awake I would tell them that the fish went down into his cave, where all those stars shone so brightly in the blue water, and he looked at them, and he closed his eyes and wished so hard he could reverse time, and the earth would cool, and the oceans would cover the planet again, and the stars would not burn out anymore, and he could follow their shining trails into the water and touch them with his fins again.

Instead, the fish learned to walk on land, and if ever a star did not turn to ashes on its way to earth, he collected its dark but gleaming form and cradled it gently in his fins.

When I go back outside and crawl into my own sleeping bag, Rachel opens her eyes and says, "Where'd you go?"

"I had to say good night to Dad."

"Oh." She squinches down until only her eyes and the top of her head show, so when she speaks up again her voice is muffled. "Mom?"

"Yeah, sweetie?"

"Tell me the story again."

"Which story?"

"You know. *The* story."

"Again?"

"Yeah."

I sigh. "A long time ago, when I met your father, I knew right away that one day I was going to marry him."

"How did you know?"

"I knew because talking to him was like talking to me, but in an opposite world, where down is up and up is down and all the water is in the sky so the fish swim around our heads and the clouds move beneath our feet. Because he wasn't exactly like me, but he balanced me out. And it's like we were two halves of an ocean that had finally found each other."

"Is there somebody in opposite world for everybody to marry?" she asks.

"Of course there is," I say. "You'll meet your opposite somebody, someday."

"I hope so," she says. Then, "Good night, Mom."

"Night Rachie."

"I love you."

"I love you too."

I don't know how long I remain awake, but my eyes dry out from staring at the sky, and for every star I see, I make a wish that somewhere in a different world with a different outcome, where another version of myself exists, and maybe another version of him, they come true. They all come true, somehow.

I should have put my hand over his hand. I should have felt his knuckles in my palm. I should have leaned over, like I wanted but didn't know it yet, and planted a kiss on his perfect lips. He should have kissed me back. He should have tasted like apple cider. Our mouths should have been wet and soft against each other, unmoving, held still, with just enough pressure to let us know that we were still there, still alive, still kissing by that lake with the water at our ankles, while the stars scattered through the open sky.

And when we went to sleep in our tents, the Perseids should have flown over us and dashed themselves onto the granite shore where we'd been sitting. A fish should have climbed out of the water on his tail fin, looked at the cold ring of stones where the campfire had been, collected the stars, and slipped back into the lake without a sound.

PHILEMATOPHILIA

BATRACHOPHILIA

The fact of the matter is that it was a perfect afternoon, and the waterfowl were upon the water, green heads gleaming and little ducklings all paddling in a row, and the birds were in the trees or the birds were in the sky, and if they were in the trees they were roosting among the branches dappled gold and they were making roosting sounds, and if they were in the sky they were darting here and there like winks or if by two, blinks, and they were fast and free and their calls were all the more so, and the songs that came from them were flashes of bright against the thin blue air, and the wind in the rushes and over the lake and carpets of green grass was sweet as springwater and cold as clay and if it touched you, and it touched everything that day, you felt like all of your nerve ends had been switched on, and there you were, there everything was electric and firing and alive.

So when Helena kissed that bullfrog, she didn't do it because he swore he was royalty. She did it because watching the reflection of clouds in the lake was like watching cream being poured into a blue cup. She did it because he was a talking frog! And how often do you meet a talking frog. And how often is the afternoon perfect like that, with the faraway mountains looking so much like footstools, like you could just longjump the valley and land that close to the sky.

It didn't matter that the frog had not lied, and he really was a prince, and he was handsome, and kind, but she already knew that, and when the dust settled there were sparkles resting in his hair and when he stood the sunlight glanced off every part of him.

He was grateful, and he offered to marry her, but she didn't even know his name, so she said, "No, but thank you," and the Frog Prince went naked into the hills toward the faraway mountains.

OPTOPHILIA

What she will do is: when you are sleeping, she will put her lip to your crow's feet. She will put her lip to the corner of your eye, whether you have crow's feet or not. She will like the edge of your lashline against her philtrum. Even before you're a baby, and you're sent down to earth from heaven, Peter or maybe some other gatekeeper puts his finger just there, just so, so that you forget, you forget, and all you have left is that hush mark from an angel's finger.

For Helena, it's not about the dark and it's not about the light. It's about the feeling of opening like window shades being rolled up and how in the quiet grey-blue overcast daylight everything looks queer and perfectly centered. It's about air, dizziness, when she raises her eyelids, and her eyes are not focused and there is a split second of headache, when she is uncertain of where she is and what that means is that she is anywhere and unsettled for just one sliver of time.

When she was in seventh grade at her first boy-girl party, and the boys were by the punch bowl like wild young zebras stomping their feet and slurping unspiked drinks, and the girls were by the stereo humming electrically, they all wanted to play Spin the Bottle or Seven Minutes in Heaven, and they didn't play Spin the Bottle.

In the closet among the winterwear, shins knocking against the vacuum cleaner, with an orange crack of light on her ankles, Helena could hear Mariah Carey through the door, whistling the high notes. Her first kiss was all lips and no hands, though soon enough she learned to hold the back of his neck, she learned to finger his hair. How long are seven minutes, she didn't remember.

But somewhere around thirty seconds she lost her balance and her ankle caught on snowboots or a black umbrella and she held onto the boy's arm for balance and they went leaning into the rainslickers. Tinkling of metal coathangers. His back against the wall and her chest on his chest, thighs and smiles pressed, and if she could have opened her eyes then, if the others had thrown open the door six minutes early and cast Mariah Carey and Christmas lights fully on them, then she would have seen him like no one had seen him before: afraid, but happy, with his heart dancing around in him like a butterfly in a big net. But they didn't, and before seven minutes were up, there in the closet dark, Helena opened her eyes and put her hands to the sides of his face and she put her lip to the edge of his closed eye.

PHALLAINOPHILIA

She dreams underwater dreams, where breathing is heavy. How is it that you can be so weightless and so weighted down at the same time, all that water buoying you and stifling you at once. She wishes she had thicker skin, wishes she could cut up tires and stitch them together into a coat or something. She likes that idea, being made of tires, of things that carry you forward.

Have you ever been in water so murky or deep that when you look down you can't see the bottom, but you can see the illusion of bottom, where the skylight strikes downward and gets lost, and as you're imagining seafloor you're sure that at any moment now something will come lunging out of those depths.

It's like that in underwater dreams except there's no fear, and she is sure that whatever comes for her will feel like a happily ever after, however many teeth, however dead and bulbous the cast-iron eyes. For now, she's more entranced to be breathing at all, to have her body up-down slightly at the pull of the moon, or is it the shudder of the earth. She's mesmerized by the silverbright of the surface from below, how the waves are sharp and cut each other sideways, how the sun hits the water like a rocket.

When it does come, rising monstrous in froth and dramatic pressure changes, she climbs onto its back, holds it between her thighs like a horse, though it's so much more than a horse, puts her palms to the stovebolts of its nose, and they dive.

Deep sea pressure can be a killer, but there in the dark it's just her and this creature with fins like wings. She puts her cheek to it and squeezes her eyes shut against the feeling that her skull will soon cave.

She just holds on and goes deep, with all that water crushing her, compacting her, until she is no longer hollow, until she is far enough away from the sky now, compressed enough now that she is no bigger than the very dense head of a pin, and she doesn't have to feel so depleted and empty and alone.

KENOPHILIA

I was like that once, I was like Helena, once. I used to think, maybe I'm a conduit, a copper pipe or a conductor cable for some force beamed down to earth via satellite, and I wasn't talking about aliens, I think I was talking about angels, and there were brief moments when I was full and the entirety of existence was flowing through me, but then the moment was over, and I was empty and echoing again, and nothing, nothing at all had changed.

ANABLEPHILIA

The thing about having eyes on the top of your head is that you don't have to crane your neck in order to look at the sky. When he was just Prince, when he was just human, the Frog Prince had been plagued by incessant neck pain, by migraine and headache, by stubbed toes and bruised shins. Quite the character he appeared, crown askew, grass stains on his knees and scratched palms, always halfway off-balance with looking up.

It didn't matter whether there were clouds or stars or birds up there, or not. Expansive unchanging blue and he'd still have his cleft chin pointing at the sun.

You'd have thought being bound in the body of a frog was a punishment, you'd have thought so, but maybe the Witch wasn't so wicked as we all thought. Now Frog Prince likes spending his days with his legs splayed over a lily pad, sitting still as a rock, staring up.

"Wouldn't you have rather been a bird?" Helena asks one day. Flat on her back in the green grass, arms spread over her head, watching nothing. "Like a falcon? Or even a sparrow?"

Frog Prince doesn't look at her, just says, his large mouth barely or slowly opening, "That's not the same."

"Well yeah," she laughs. "If you're a bird, you're actually in the sky."

"But it was never about that." He blinks carefully and his eyes become more golden and his oblong pupils wider or darker. He doesn't say anything more, but what he means is that it's about the feeling of being stretched between your feet and your gaze in the air, being drawn out in a line between these.

"If I met the Witch, I'd want to be a shark. Or an alligator."

"No, you wouldn't."

"No, not really." Helena sighs. "I just like teeth."

Here Frog Prince looks slyly at her out of the corners of his big round eyes. If round eyes have corners. "Did you know, toads don't have teeth."

"Do frogs?"

"Maxillary teeth," he says proudly and bares his row of tiny serrations for her to see. She wants to lean over the water and run the tip of her finger along them, just brush the top of his mouth.

"They're tiny," she says. "They're cute."

Helena passes her tongue over her front teeth, feeling their flatness like tiles. Frog Prince watches her, watches her tongue move beneath her upper lip, flattening out her cupid's bow, and for the first time in years he wants to be human again. He wants to leap onto her chest, and he knows he could make the jump. He has faith in his back legs. He wants to put his webs on the curves of her breasts and sit there and have her upper lip underneath his right hand.

He wants to maybe put his frog lips to hers and flick his frog tongue into the pink cavern of her mouth.

Standing now, head tilted, neck long like a giraffe or a bridge, Helena asks, like she's reading his mind, which she isn't, "Do you ever miss being human?" She can feel the sky on her throat, sliding down her spine and into the cup of her heart. What she's thinking is Frog Prince doesn't get to feel that, not with the way his frog body is, crouched up like that, all curled with no thoroughfare for the sky to get into the edges of him, and despite the neck pain and the stubbed toes, maybe that's what it is about looking up, not just seeing.

NOMATOPHILIA

You can't live in a town this small, in a community so pinched in on itself, and not have them whisper about you when you walk by. You can't walk into a deli and order a Coke or a turkey sandwich without having ladies with their hair in tinfoil, wearing shiny black capes, abandon their hairdryers and sneak in from the salon next door, only to say while your back is turned, "Did you hear…," hoping you will be compelled to relate the truth in the rumor.

They started when she was fourteen, just into high school. She played flute and there was a boy who played bassoon, his name was Mark, and he had dark hair and dandruff, braces, and a shy smile like he was never sure if while he was smiling Helena was going to turn into a toad or maybe a tortoise, though maybe he still would have been entranced by her if she had.

They'd been holding hands at lunch for a month. They'd been holding hands after school for two weeks, and she would lay belly-down on his bed, chin propped on her elbows and her feet kicking up in the air, poring over *Great Expectations* or a brief section of science textbook on metamorphic rocks while he sat upright at his desk doing algebra, or maybe just watching her.

The truth is that on that mid-October afternoon, his sheets were ripples and she liked the folds of them under her hands. Outside the grass was browning and the driveway was pale concrete and cracked, and she wasn't reading that day, just looking back at him.

He leaned over, awkwardly, and when he kissed her his braces scraped against her teeth.

She felt like a balloon whose string had been cut, and she was soaring up past his second-story window and through the clingy branches of the oak tree shading half the house, and she was still going up, past telephone wires and radio towers, and she was sure that the air was thin and she was going to pop.

But she was also still in the room, and she smiled at him, and she put her hands on the back of his neck and she jerked him off the chair and she half-fell off the bed and he was crouched there on the carpet looking bewildered but intensely happy when she put her mouth against his mouth.

Two days later at his orthodontist appointment, while his rubber bands were being changed, while his mouth was growing dry and his lips were chapping and the side of his head was pushed uncomfortably close to the chest of the slant-eyed dental hygienist—he thought she must be some exotic mix of Indo-European descent, some lithe, bronzy creature beneath those scrubs—Mark's doctor told him, It's a miracle, Mark, I don't know how it happened, I'm good but I'm not God, and this has got to be some sort of divine intervention, because your teeth are the straightest teeth I have ever seen. You don't need braces, I don't see why we can't just take them off now and fit you for a retainer.

Seven days later the second-chair clarinetist was running her fingers over his skull and saying how soft his hair is, how shiny, what conditioner do you use?

Maybe you know the rest. Maybe you know that on the eighth day Mark told Helena that it's not her, it's him, and this was true, because what an asshole, ditching her, ditching even the bassoon for shin guards and soccer practice instead, to sit across the quad with the second-chair clarinetist and her twin sister, the soprano section leader in choir.

Maybe you know that it wasn't too long before Bobby, before Chris and Darren and another Chris, before these and more were lining up because what they said while pissing next to each other in the boys' locker room is that, Man, you won't believe it till you try it, she'll change your life.

She stopped Bobby's stutter, she fixed Chris #2's lazy eye, she got Darren an A in English and decades later a position as Poet Laureate of New Jersey, and over the course of four years as she kissed each member of the basketball team, they went from last in the league as freshmen to state champions as varsity players. And you can't kiss this many boys, you can't change this many people, and have that go unnoticed.

So when she enters the house this morning, this early hour of 5:30 a.m., her step-mother is standing in the foyer, in a bathrobe, in wrinkled and loosening skin. Her hair, dry and graying and coming free from the bun at the back of her neck. The displeased purse of her lips, thin and snapped closed. Because when she goes to the post office to pick up her packages, the postmaster, a woman with a chest like a shelf and clumping mascara, snidely says, Who is it this week? Imagine this happening all over town. Imagine step-mother's shame and possibly envy, because no one would ever think that her kisses could change you like that, though maybe once, a long time ago, if she ever was beautiful or kissable, they could have.

So when Helena enters the house this morning, this early hour of 5:30 a.m., step-mother has only one thing to say, and she fastens it around Helena's neck like a chain, and it burns like a cattlebrand, and though she'll maybe carry that scar for the rest of her life, because we all know that sticks and stones are only sticks and stones, Helena sits on the fraying or fading Persian rug and puts her hand to her throat, her fingertips on her neck, feeling the edges of that word, sharp points and sliding surfaces. She likes the way it sparkles and sends barbs of light in all directions. Red, vicious light. She puts the word to her lips, holds it there for a minute before opening her mouth and putting it in. She rolls it over with her tongue, coats it in saliva, bites at it with her molars. SLUT. Swallows.

NYCTOHYLOPHILIA

The Beast found her at night in a clearing of sugar pines, sitting cross-legged on a flat-topped granite boulder, with pools of dark mulchy needles in the grass. She was staring into the forest, and she had not seen him yet, but he had seen her, elbows on her knees, gazing at the trees with an intensity and fascination that he had only seen on the faces of scholars at books or predators stalking prey, but with a joy that transformed her face entirely, so that she was neither academician nor animal, but a different, more alive creature altogether.

He said, "Don't be afraid," and remained in the shadows behind her.

Helena didn't even turn to find him, even if she could have found him, camouflaged as he was in his spotted or maybe striped pelt. "I'm not afraid," she replied, and she wasn't. Helena had an addiction to truth the way some people are addicted to punctuality. Physically unable to tell lies, to be late.

"Are you lost?" asked the Beast. Deep rumble like the engine of an ocean liner. With coal burning inside.

"Maybe," she said, "but it doesn't matter."

The Beast crept to the edge of the clearing, soundless, the way hunting animals are, though he was not hunting, not hungry or desperate, just curious. "Why not?" he asked.

"Because I want to be here."

Truth be told, she liked the way the tree trunks seemed flat against the dark of the woods and how they rose up and up and up until they became flat against the sky. She liked how the forest sounds became sharp and meaningful in the night. She wanted to be like that: sharp and meaningful.

Helena was not afraid when the Beast sat down beside her, not afraid of the dirty, oily smell of his fur or the tatters that remained of his clothing.

"I've heard about you," she said, looking down at his claws. She wanted to touch them.

"What did you hear?" She was such a small thing. He could snap her in half, if he wanted to, but he didn't.

"Do you eat people?"

"No, but I eat animals. If I'm one of them now, does that make me a cannibal?"

Helena looked at him then. If she recognized some part of herself in him, in those cream-colored horns, in the hackles stiff-raised along his spine, some part of her that had generations ago forgotten how to be human and how not to divorce from the animal body, she didn't know it. She just knew she liked the question; it made her wonder at her own animalness, if she had any.

"Are you really an animal?" she asked.

"No."

What the Beast explained to her then was that he used to be a man, a prince, even, and when he kissed the first enchanted sleeper, he hadn't done it because he wanted a wife and he hadn't done it because she was beautiful. "They're always beautiful," he said, but he'd done it because it wasn't right that someone with all that life left to live should sleep through it, while thorny vines swallowed her castle and everyone she knew grew old and died. He'd done it because he'd come all this way, and it wasn't right for him to leave her there.

Her lips were cold and rubbery and he was tired and his arm was broken from the fight with the dragon or maybe a den of lions, and it wasn't at all romantic. He knelt and put his lips to hers, and it was awkward, but it was enough, because she opened her eyes and threw her arms around his neck and wanted him on or in her, but he was tired and his arm was broken and she didn't understand. So he said, "No, but thank you," and Sleeping Beauty stood up and the Beast recalls now how she opened the curtains and how the sunlight was blinding, but in a good way.

When Helena touched his paw, then, where it rested on the granite between them, she saw his fur melt back into the few soft hairs of human hands. She saw his black talons recede and flatten and fade into the transparency of human fingernails. Then, as she held his hand, she looked into his face, and she saw there a human face, not the face of a beast, horned and snouted and baring fangs, but a man's face with five o'clock shadows in the planes of his cheeks and thick eyebrows but straight except for an arch of intelligence, or maybe it was confidence, and epic Greco-Roman lips like those carved out of marble, only his were moving.

"Why did the Witch turn you into a Beast, then?" she asked.

"Who knows?" the Beast said. "The Witch works in mysterious ways. I keep hoping one day, when the time is right, I'll turn back." He sighed, and looked sad, and wilted a little bit. "Or maybe not," he added as an afterthought, "maybe this is just who I am now."

"It's not," Helena said. "It's not. It's not." And she was crying, not wanting to believe that she could see all of his possibilities, all of his virtues there before her in the night, but that he might never become this man she knew he could be, and she was so overcome that she kissed him then, and what she saw became what he was. And he offered to marry her, but it was enough to see him standing there shedding his old clothing and his old skin, feeling new and shiny in his human body, loving the sky on him, unmediated by fur.

DENDROPHILIA

I used to dream about your forearms. In my head they were spindly like branches, and smooth, if not soft, and what I wanted to do was hold them; I wanted to wrap my fingers around them, half-way between your wrists and the fleshy bend of your elbow, I wanted to wrap my fingers around your forearms like vines. I just wanted to hold them.

I would dream about that part of your face where your nose and your cheek connect, that soft square of skin below the inside corner of your eye. I imagined our foreheads pressed, eyes downcast not out of sorrow but because they were closing, lashes sweeping skin, this like nuzzling, like some quiet animal sort of intimacy. I wanted to kiss your eyebrow. I liked how close I was to your bones. I wanted put my face to your face.

I used to dream about your knuckles, but only if your hands were laid flat or your fingers were extended. I thought of your palms as smooth and lined like woodgrain. And your knuckles were knots and the more I touched them, the smoother they would become. I wanted to take the big knuckle of your forefinger, where it connected to your palm, I wanted to take it in my mouth and suck on it like a stick of licorice root, prodding it with the tongue and testing it lightly with the teeth.

MICROPHILIA

Unless the Witch seeks you out—and if she does she will find you wherever you are and it's okay to be empty-handed when she does, for she will not expect that you have come with payment, but if you are holding, for example, a fishbowl or a small terrarium she will take it from you and you will have no say in the matter—you are to collect one blue stone, no bigger than your fist but no smaller than the tip of your thumb, and it is imperative that you find this stone yourself—she will know if you haven't—and: a strip of green plastic, a sticker of Saturn, the celestial body not the god and preferably glow-in-the-dark, a bottle of springwater, recyclable, and a porcelain figurine. These are the tokens she will require, and you can be sure that she will not show up if you don't have them, that is, unless she seeks you out first.

When you have your stone, your length of green, your planet, your bottled water, and your little deep sea diver or treasure chest, you must put them in a carrying sack—a paper bag will work—and go to a hill facing due west, covered 97% with grass, not necessarily cultivated or even green, and having a 30° to 45° incline.

Then you wait.

They say, speaking loudly over the sound of the domed hair dryers, Did you know, your crotch can rot from overuse? What they don't say, what they never said, and what Helena did not expect was that after the Beast, after she had kissed enough men to wonder why when they left her they were full of electricity, why they were improved when they left her, why she never felt changed the way they did, and after she stopped kissing them altogether because she could not stand to feel so charged, while her mouth was open and her lips were supple, and then after, so empty and unchanged, what she did not expect was to forget. She forgot, because after moving away, she kissed no one for years, for decades maybe, who knew, while she waited on the hillside, facing west, with the birds in the trees or the birds in the sky, talking politics and religion with the Frog Prince, forgetting what it was like to kiss, to be channeling a beam of energy sent straight through her from the sky, to be filled like that or even to be emptied the way she used to be, and it got harder and harder to pretend that she remembered any of it, that she hadn't grown solid and cold in her center.

APEIROPHILIA

The fact of the matter is that it had nothing to do with the birds or the trees or the movement of air across the water. It was like this:

When I got to you, you were standing there in the snow, with your sneakers all damp and your feet sliding out from under you. You were white or pink with cold. I was shivering. It was winter, and the sky was a bedsheet drawn over our heads. I didn't know what to do. I forgot how to say hello. How to shake your hand.

Did you look at me and was I just as you imagined?

When I got to you, there was a carousel and painted ponies and paper masks, and everyone was wearing mittens. Red scarves. When I got to you, I was as sharply defined as coal in snow.

It was a Friday afternoon. There were pigeons or blackbirds on the telephone wires, and when they launched into the sky, their stick-feet sent blips of sound into the thin January air. Flakes of snow or pearls of music drifting over my fingertips as I reached for them. You laughed, maybe. Are you frightened by perfection? The trees were naked.

I kissed you. One day, I'm going to forget everything else, but I'm not going to forget the way you came toward me. Like a slow rocket or a fast rocket in slow motion, with the horses in the background and all those hands waving, all those mouths open. I'm not going to forget the way you looked at me and I'm going to remember how it felt to look at you, through the fog of the world, which had been waiting for us, for this, which was holding its breath or standing still, and all its ears and all its eyes were turned toward us, toward that square of sidewalk where our toes nearly touched.

It had everything to do with the world, conspiring toward that moment, but ultimately outside of us, looking in on that singularity. Where we were standing so close. Where the birds and the wind dropped away soundlessly. Where we became infinite. Everything at once intimately connected and altogether foreign, and it had everything and nothing to do with us.

I reached up and took your face in my hands. I pressed my mouth to yours and I opened you up with my tongue. You kissed me. You held on to me in such a way that I was in your arms and yet I was in the rhythm of the telephone wires, I was in the teeth of plastic ponies and in the lines of the concrete and deeper. We were alight from the inside, electricity or breath running between us and out of us into the naked trees. Remember the glowing streets, how bright it was, and how, afterwards, the direction of everything was changed, how we were able to see the slant of snow falling and how the freeways embraced the curvature of the earth, we were able to discern the movements of crowds and flickering of fluorescent bulbs as they turned on, the line of a pencil the same as the line of a wooden bridge the same as the cold creek it crossed and the crisp edge of a slice of whole grain wheat as it appeared from the mouth of a toaster in Weatherby Lake, Missouri.

ICHTHYOPHILIA

When the Wicked Witch arrives, her torso is a fishbowl, and inside is blue gravel, a length of plastic seaweed, and a little orange goldfish, whose eyes are brighter than marbles or planets on dark nights, whose fins are small but sharp and flick him from one side of the bowl to the other, swimming in figure eights, drinking in everything he can see and more that he cannot, with every rhythmic pulse of his gills.

He sees a woman, sitting on the edge of the pond, her bare legs dangling in the water, pale beneath the surface and sending ripples to the farther shore. She's laughing. She's got a laugh that bursts out of her like an ignited match. You can maybe smell phosphorus, if you're not underwater.

He sees a frog, patterned with black, slick with moisture, smiling slyly or shyly, and gazing so adoringly up at this woman. One eye on the sky and the other on her face, resting on her parted lips.

"Kiss me," he says, finally. It's been years. Dreaming of this.

"What?"

"Kiss me."

Helena stops laughing. "I can't," she says.

"You can. You have to."

I don't remember how, she wants to say. Even if I wanted to, I don't remember how.

"It's not because I want to be human again. It's not because I want to feel something." It's because if I don't kiss you, now, I don't know if I'll ever get the chance again, and I don't want my life to be empty of you like that.

Frog Prince ducks into the water. It's cold, and he likes the way the light spiderwebs over him. He kicks once, twice, with strong kicks from his back legs. Elegant and quick underwater, looking more human than Helena has ever seen him.

He leaps onto the bank, places one webbed paw on her knee, on her thigh, and he looks up into her face.

She picks him up with both hands. She holds him so that they are eye-level. "Kiss me," she says.

When their lips meet, she's falling into the grass, unrolling like a carpet, until she is flat and trembling, with Frog Prince at her mouth, hard frog lips and tiny frog teeth nipping at her, tongue flicking in and out of her, caressing her gums, the insides of her cheeks.

When their lips meet, the Frog Prince has his legs on her collarbone, his hands on her jaw, belly against her chin. Until he is growing, and his knees are grass-bound on either side of her, and he's holding himself up at the elbows with his fingers in her hair.

All this, the Witch and her goldfish heart see. She raps her knuckles on the bowl, lightly, affectionately, and smiles. He does a flip and watches as Helena and the Prince part.

But he doesn't see Helena's heart quiver, glowing orange and splitting down the middle, hatching a small tadpole in the chamber of her chest, so that when the Prince takes her hand and says, "Will you marry me?", she feels the tadpole stir and swim through her veins, and she is not empty anymore—because she never was, not really—and though she loves him, she won't say yes, not now, because she doesn't need to, and can you imagine years from now when her heart is fully grown and kicking its back legs elegantly and fluidly and looking up?

ACKNOWLEDGMENTS

Sections of this collection previously appeared, in various incarnations, in the following publications: *Prick of the Spindle, Thieves Jargon, Toasted Cheese, ABJECTIVE, Able Muse*, and *The Big Stupid Review*.

I would like to thank my friends and family for their love and support, and this collection would not have been possible without the work and insight of my colleagues and instructors at UC Santa Cruz and San Francisco State. In particular, I need to extend enormous thanks to the following: Mom, Chris, Steve, Nina, Alice, Dodie, Peter, Vinh, and Cole. Thank you for supporting me, for inspiring me, for guiding me, for showing me how to break the rules, and for never telling me that it wasn't possible, that it wasn't practical, that it wasn't worth doing. Because it is.

In keeping with one of the motifs of the collection, many of these stories are inspired by music. Some explicitly reference songs and lyrics, but others have music interwoven directly into their structures and sentences. What follows is a list of the artists and songs that have influenced the collection.

"Fish Songs"

Bomb the Music Industry. "Big Plans of Sleeping In" and "Ready... Set... No!!!" *Album Minus Band.* 2005.

---. "Stand There 'Til You're Sober" and "Skye! Life Is Awesome!" *To Leave or Die in Long Island.* 2007.

---. "I Don't Love You Anymore." *Get Warmer.* 2007.

"Down (Down Down)"

Streetlight Manifesto. "Down Down Down to Mephisto's Café" and "What a Wicked Gang Are We." *Somewhere in the Between.* 2007.

"The Fisherman"

Imogen Heap. "Hide and Seek." *Speak for Yourself.* 2005.

"Not the Same"

Ben Folds. "Not the Same." *Rockin' the Suburbs.* 2001.

The Beach Boys. "God Only Knows." *Pet Sounds.* 1966.

"Over and Over and Over"

Sprout. "Straight to the Core." *Victim of the Green.* 2000.

Rocky Votolato. "Suicide Medicine." *Suicide Medicine.* 2003.

"Derek"

Suburban Legends. "Bright Spring Morning." *Dance Like Nobody's Watching.* 2006.

"To Keep Me Awake and Alive"

Peter Gabriel. "In Your Eyes." *So.* 1986.

"Anatomy of the Human Heart"

Journey. "Don't Stop Believin'." *Escape*. 1981.

The Beatles. "When I'm Sixty-Four." *Sgt. Pepper's Lonely Hearts Club Band*. 1967.

Queen. "Somebody to Love." *A Day at the Races*. 1976.

"Philematophilia"

Plushgun. "Just Impolite." *Pins & Panzers*. 2009.

ABOUT THE AUTHOR

Traci Chee is a freelance writer with a degree in Creative Writing from San Francisco State University. Her work has most recently been published by *The Big Stupid Review, ABJECTIVE,* and *Prick of the Spindle.* She likes fish and ships.

CPSIA information can be obtained at www.ICGtesting.com
Printed in the USA
LVOW021603130513

333561LV00006B/8/P